Justice

Georges Simenon
JUSTICE

TRANSLATED FROM THE FRENCH BY
GEOFFREY SAINSBURY

A Helen and Kurt Wolff Book

HARCOURT BRACE JOVANOVICH, PUBLISHERS

SAN DIEGO   NEW YORK   LONDON

Library of Congress Cataloging in Publication Data

Simenon, Georges, 1903–
  Justice.

  Translation of: Cour d' assises.
  "A Helen and Kurt Wolff book."
  I. Title.
PQ2637.I53C6313   1985   843'.912   85–855
ISBN 0–15–146585–1

Designed by G. B. D. Smith

Printed in the United States of America

First American edition

A B C D E

Justice

1

FOR ALL THE OTHERS who were there, all except Petit Louis, there was nothing exceptional on the earth or in the sky, nothing but a rosy, luminous evening like any other at Le Lavendou, when every object was thrown into sharp relief by the clarity of the air under a sky that was growing cold. A scene that was picturesque enough—a memory to be treasured along with those shells and picture postcards that record the history of summer vacations.

How good it was to be alive!

At the bottom of the hilly street, the shady square by the harbor still sported its decorations for Bastille Day, July 14, the palms were a sumptuous green in the light of the setting sun, and the flags hung as motionless as if painted on a backcloth.

And nobody realized, as the red of sunset spread halfway across the sky and the blue in the other half gradually turned to green, as sounds became sharper, suddenly swelling, then as suddenly dying as though appalled by their incongruity, nobody realized that that moment—an ordinary moment for all the world to enjoy—belonged really to Petit Louis and to no one else, all the others being merely supers.

On the beach, near the casino and the diving board, a few people still lingered, lying stretched out on the sand. Mothers sauntered homeward, dragging little children in bright-colored bathing suits.

Now and again a car would drive down the street, and then there would be a slamming of doors and cries of greeting as figures in white joined the other figures in white already sitting at the little tables in front of the Potinière.

Petit Louis's eyes were laughing, only his eyes, as happens at those rare and happy moments of our existence when we know with absolute certainty that whatever we do is bound to succeed. They laughed as they glanced at the post office clock, whose hands were at exactly two minutes to seven. And they laughed as they wandered caressingly over the front of the Hôtel Provençal, dwelling for a moment on one of the second-floor windows.

There must have been about twenty people gathered around him in an admiring circle, passers-by who stopped for a minute or two to watch him play, women in flowered bathing suits who were returning from the beach with their bags of knitting, men who were intrigued by his display of skill, local fishermen in their loose trousers that hung limply from their hips.

It had begun four days earlier, when Petit Louis had first gone into the Café du Centre. He was wearing the same light-gray suit, very light indeed, and the same fancy shoes, partly leather, partly snakeskin. Close-shaved and powdered, he walked with a sort of cautious buoyancy, like people on Sunday mornings who find themselves once more in their clean clothes and walk carefully, avoiding the stones and glancing self-consciously at their reflection in shop windows.

In the café were all sorts, from fishermen to vacationers. Ignoring them, Petit Louis concentrated his attention on a slot machine, into which he slipped one coin after another until finally the kitty fell in a cascade of one-franc pieces, which rolled all over the floor.

A windfall. But he accepted it as though it was only his due. He wandered outside, where a group of locals were playing bowls near some drying fishing nets. They were talking vociferously, to show off in front of the handful of visitors looking on.

Petit Louis didn't say much. Merely:

"Let me have your balls a minute, pal."

He threw one twenty-five yards away. Then with the other he took aim, stepped three paces backward, ran three paces forward, and the ball hit the first one with a hard, dry knock. All the players turned to look at him.

It was then that the laughter had come into his eyes. The adventure had only started, and started exactly as he had planned. Half an hour later he was engaged in a match with the others, in front of a crowd of onlookers that got thicker every moment.

"Are you from Marseille?" asked one of the fishermen.

Petit Louis wasn't very communicative.

"Somewhere around there . . ."

Some boys between fifteen and eighteen looked enviously at his white flannel cap, his shoes with pointed toes, and the ring he wore on his left hand. Some men, who might have been Parisians, exchanged ironical glances and moved on, but their wives lingered to watch him.

"Who's your crack player?" he asked next day.

He challenged him and won. Then he took on the postmaster, Monsieur Bauche, from whom he won fifty francs.

"I'll give you the chance for revenge on Monday, in the street outside the Provençal."

"All right. But not before seven."

And now the stage was set. Two minutes to seven. One minute to. To warm up, Petit Louis was playing against a garage man and one of the cooks of the Provençal. It didn't occur to anybody to wonder why he'd chosen such a place for the match. It was right at a cross street, where they were disturbed by every passing car. Under the trees in the square, they'd have been in nobody's way.

Just below them, a solitary car was drawn up against the curb, not far from the bazaar, whose windows were packed with hoops, bathing suits, and toy balloons.

"Here he comes!"

Monsieur Bauche had already taken off his jacket, and as he walked along, he weighed his balls in his hands, as though he fully appreciated the importance of the contest.

"Are you standing by the odds you offered?" he asked.

"A hundred francs to ten."

The laughter in Petit Louis's eyes shone still more strongly, while the onlookers repeated the stakes and a figure disappeared from one of the upstairs windows.

"It's your start. . . . Throw the jack. . . ."

A pageboy, the hall porter, and the receptionist of the Provençal watched the game from the hotel steps. The revolving doors turned. Petit Louis betrayed no curiosity, but he knew that a woman came out, fascinated by the spectacle, and edged her way into the front row.

As though to reward her, he took a shot at twenty yards and brought off an *estanque*. Then he gave her a look, as much as to say:

"There you are! . . . Is that what you wanted?"

But, Heaven knows, he had other things to think about. The minutes that passed were becoming more and more momentous. He took in everything: the big car drawn up by the curb, another car on the right-hand side of the road, two men smoking cigarettes in the back row of the crowd, above all, the big hand of the clock and the red face of the postmaster, who blamed the stones on the ground each time he missed.

"Three to nothing . . . I'll give you ten points as a handicap, if you like, Monsieur Bauche."

The woman was almost too earnest, too optimistic, too melting. It almost put Petit Louis off his stroke, for he couldn't help glancing at her after every throw to see her reaction.

He knew nothing about her except that she was staying at

the Provençal—that is to say, at the best hotel—that she was all alone, and that she wore the minimum of clothing, showing patches of sunburn on her soft fat shoulders.

The evening before, he had jokingly said to her:

"Step back a little, will you, Mama?"

But seeing her mortification, he had made up for it by a radiant smile.

She might be fifty, perhaps more, but she had nonetheless fallen for Petit Louis, and never failed to appear from somewhere or other the moment he had the balls in his hands. And there she stood gaping, hypnotized to such an extent that she had to be pushed out of the way for a car to pass.

"Just watch me while I do a *palet!*"

His three inimitable steps, or leaps . . . and the ball described a flat parabola and struck his adversary's clean in the middle. . . .

The post office was a small building at a corner, with one entrance at the front and another on the side street. The windows were barred. A mailbox was fixed to the pink wall.

One of the assistants, the older one, came out. She was from Paris, and lived with her mother in a family pension. Then the younger one left, the one who squinted. The evening before, Petit Louis had, just to pass the time, kidded with her.

"Of course, if you're a professional . . ." grumbled the postmaster, disheartened.

It was just at that moment that everything happened, and it was funny to see Monsieur Bauche's mustache quivering with annoyance, while behind the spectators, and hidden by them, two men forced their way into the post office.

In spite of himself, Petit Louis's mind wandered for a moment from the game. He lit a cigarette to regain his composure. Then, with an affected nonchalance, he leaped forward and threw his ball.

"That'll do it."

The words slipped out. He would have done better to wait, because he lost the point. He frowned; his admirer put on a pained expression to show her sympathy.

"Oh, well! . . . It'll have to be the next one."

But he lost that, too, and a triumphant smile spread over Monsieur Bauche's face. He wiped his forehead as he walked back with his balls, and he couldn't refrain from making a dig at Petit Louis.

"Thought it was in the bag, did you?"

With one glance, Petit Louis took in the post office and the square, with its shady trees and its flags for July 14 lighted by the setting sun.

The hands of the clock were at eight minutes past seven. And once more he missed his shot, frowned, and roughly pushed aside a boy who laughed at him.

"My point!" cried Monsieur Bauche.

But nothing mattered any longer now, as Petit Louis knew by the sound of an engine accelerating. The spectators squeezed to one side to let a car pass, then another, after which they resumed their places in a rectangle around the players. It was the postmaster's turn, and his ball stopped within an inch of the jack.

Petit Louis felt he must do something startling. He turned to his admirer.

"Would you like to have a drink on it? . . . That I'll drive him off it first shot? . . ."

She nodded, too thrilled to speak.

"You're not going to score another point, Monsieur Bauche," he boasted as he crouched to make his shot.

"We'll see about that. . . ."

"All right, look at this. . . ."

And once more his balls hit his opponent's fairly and squarely.

"What's your score now?" he asked.

"Three," answered the postmaster.

"Well, if you score another point, a single one, we'll call the match yours."

From that moment he could do as he liked. He was absolutely sure of himself. The balls obeyed his will. He hardly bothered to aim.

6

"Thirteen . . ."

"Fourteen . . ."

"And now for the winning shot . . ."

"Not that one!"

"Wait till it stops. . . . There! . . . What did I tell you?"

As at a football game, it was no sooner over than the crowd began to disintegrate, each person resuming his own life, his own personality.

"I've left my money behind," said Monsieur Bauche. "I'll go and get it."

"No hurry . . . Whenever you like . . ."

"No. I've lost the match, and we'll settle up at once."

Women drifted into the grocery, others to the terrace of the nearest café, until there was no one left near Petit Louis but his admirer, whose ample bosom fluttered under a flowered scarf knotted behind her neck.

"Well?"

"I owe you a drink."

"All right, let's go."

She could hardly believe it was true. But it was. She was really walking beside him, and, when they got to the terrace of the Potinière, he offered her a chair with quite unexpected gallantry.

"Sit down. . . . It won't be long before we see the postmaster."

He simply couldn't help it. The temptation was irresistible, and he added:

"He'll be in a hell of a state, I'm sure."

"Why?"

They were interrupted by the waiter.

"*Menthe* and water," ordered Petit Louis. "And yours, Madame?"

"It's all the same to me. . . . I'll have one, too. . . . You were saying?"

"Nothing . . . How long have you been staying in Le Lavendou?"

"Only a week. And I'm bored with it already. I don't like the people. . . ."

She held out her cigarette case, then a gold lighter, which he couldn't refrain from keeping for a moment in his hand to feel its weight.

"I suppose they're what you might call family people," he answered, staring at a table where a bearded man was surrounded by four children.

"The place is full of dressmakers."

But Petit Louis wasn't listening. He nudged her arm.

"Look!"

"Where? . . . What is it?"

The post office was around the corner, but the postmaster had come into sight, agitated and gesticulating, walking beside a policeman he'd fetched from the square.

"What's happened?"

He pressed his foot on hers, though she was wearing only sandals. There was nothing he couldn't get away with!

A few people got up and sauntered toward the post office to see what was the matter.

"Have you done something?" she whispered.

Petit Louis answered with a wink.

"But isn't it dangerous for you to stay here?"

He looked around him, and his lips curled as he sneered.

"There's nothing to stop me from staying, if you'd like to invite me to dinner."

"You know as well as I do that there's nothing I'd like better. . . . But what's going on?"

They could see the back of the crowd that was gathering at the post office.

"Come on. Let's take a stroll."

They walked the length of the square, he with his hands in his pockets and a cigarette in his mouth.

"You've been up to something, haven't you?"

"Take it easy! Don't be afraid! Everybody in the place knows

I was playing bowls. And I couldn't very well be playing bowls with the postmaster and robbing his till at the same time. . . ."

"They've robbed his . . . ?"

It was on the tip of her tongue to scold him, to say to him:

"My God! How can you be so reckless? . . ."

But Petit Louis was enjoying the calm evening air, the sky turning to a greenish tint, a red bathing suit lingering on the beach like a last vestige of a day of sunshine.

"Are you the chief?" she asked.

"Not yet."

"They're friends of yours who did it?"

"Friends of mine, yes . . . But what about dinner?"

"Where would you like to go?"

"I suppose it would hardly do to take me your hotel. . . . We might go back to the Potinière."

There were comings and goings, and always a few groups of people outside the post office. Before dinner was over, a car arrived from Hyères with some men of the flying squad, who disappeared inside.

Petit Louis was in a state of suppressed excitement. He drank nothing, not even wine, yet his cheeks were flushed and there was electricity in his fingertips.

"Tell me about yourself," pleaded his companion.

He had her on the end of his line.

"I don't know your name yet."

"Constance d'Orval . . . I'm a widow. . . ."

"I thought so."

"Why?"

"Never mind . . . Do you live in Paris?"

"No. Nice . . . I've come here just for a change of air."

"Hotel?"

"What?"

"At Nice, do you live in a hotel?"

"As a matter of fact, I have a furnished apartment. It's only temporary, until I bring my own furniture down here."

"You've got a house somewhere else?"

"Near Orléans. But life's too depressing up there for a woman all alone."

She was oozing sentimentality and was pathetically anxious to please. She positively melted in Petit Louis's presence, and tears came into her eyes.

"Now tell me what you've done."

"It's nothing to speak of. A little job that'll bring in a couple of hundred thousand."

"Two hundred thousand francs? . . . As much as that?"

"Easy. You see, there's no bank in Le Lavendou, and most of the shopkeepers bank their receipts through the post office. Then don't forget, what with July 14 and the weekend the hotels and shops must have had plenty to take in this morning."

Constance sat marveling at it all.

"The train goes at seven-thirty-two. At seven o'clock, when the post office shuts, the money's all put in bags, which are sealed, and everybody leaves except old Macagne, the winter postman, who waits there till it's time to take them to the station in his little cart."

"Have they . . . have they killed him?" she said, falteringly.

"No, no! . . . A gag over his mouth and a couple of pieces of string for his hands and feet . . ."

"Is that why you played your game of bowls just there?"

"That's right."

"Did you work it all out yourself?"

His only answer was a modest smile. A moment later, as the band struck up in the casino, she sighed.

"Won't you be suspected?"

"What if I am?"

"Suppose they arrest you?"

He went on with the game, playing his part in an offhand manner. He also played with the gold lighter, and at one moment he was on the point of slipping it in his pocket.

"When are you going to get in touch with your friends?"

"As soon as they give the signal."

"What? Are they still here?"

"No, no! . . . By this time two or three of them will be in Marseille and the rest will be scattered along the coast."

"They were driving stolen cars, weren't they?"

"I see you read the papers!"

"Are they . . . are they as young as you?"

"Titin . . . I mean, one of them is thirty-five."

"And you?"

"Twenty-four."

"You're not married?"

On the table was an electric lamp in the form of a candle, with a tiny shade of salmon-pink silk. Their neighbors on the terrace were full of the post-office raid, but Petit Louis didn't listen to them.

It must have been about eleven when he heaved a sigh and said:

"Well? Shall we go to bed?"

She was startled in spite of herself, and instinctively looked around to see if anybody had heard.

"Where?" she whispered.

"What's wrong with your hotel?"

"They'll see us going in."

"Does that bother you? . . . All right, you can go in first, and I'll join you later. What's the number of your room?"

"Number seventeen."

"I'll be there in a quarter of an hour."

He strolled out and walked up and down under the trees while she paid the bill. When she passed him, she smiled; she couldn't go nearer him without showing some sign of tenderness.

"In a quarter of an hour . . ." she murmured.

There were no more than five or six people still hanging around outside the post office. Its windows were all lighted, and a policeman stood guard at the entrance.

Petit Louis slouched into the Café du Centre and, leaning against the bar, ordered a *menthe verte*.

"What's all this business about the post office?" he asked. "It looks to me like a bright idea of the postmaster's to get out of paying me my ten francs!"

The joke fell flat, but with a shrug of his shoulders he went on:

"It'll make a great splash in the papers: The Gangsters of Le Lavendou!"

He looked around challengingly, but he knew there was nobody there anxious to take him on. Contemptuously, he threw five francs on the bar, adjusted the angle of his cap, and walked out.

A few moments later, he walked casually into the Provençal. The manager, who was doing his accounts, looked up. So did the night porter.

Petit Louis stopped, lit another cigarette, and said quietly:

"Madame d'Orval . . . Number seventeen . . . She's expecting me!"

As he put his foot on the first step, he changed his mind, and went back to the desk.

"Black coffee and croissants for me. At eight o'clock sharp."

2

LIKE SOMEONE PLAYING a trump card, Battisti let fall:

"Old Macagne's in the hospital, you know, and if he doesn't pull through, it may be awkward for you."

And Petit Louis, whose eyes still sparkled with gaiety, confined himself to a sneer.

"You don't say!"

It was continuing like those village fetes that seem as though they'd never stop. You wake up in the morning with a heavy head, but your eyes are not yet open before you remember that the fete's still on, that you can linger in bed as long as you like, while the merry-go-round gets ready for the children when they come after Mass.

The police had burst into the hotel just as Petit Louis had lit his first cigarette and started putting on his tie in front of the mirror.

"You're wanted downstairs."

"Tell them I'll be down in a second."

And to Constance, who was still in bed, with a breakfast tray on her lap:

"Get dressed quickly, Constance. . . ."

"Again?"

She was referring to her name. She had begged him to call her by her nickname, but somehow he found it difficult.

"All right, Coco," he corrected himself.

"Are you sure they'll let you go again?"

The bright, freshly painted houses made the street look like a toy bought in a bazaar. Petit Louis was escorted across it and into a building on the other side, where he found himself face to face with Inspector Battisti of the flying squad, whose path he had already crossed in Marseille. Of course Battisti was trying to unnerve him with his story of Macagne, and Petit Louis, blowing a cloud of smoke into the air, caustically answered:

"You don't say!"

"Look here, Petit Louis! Can you tell me where you've been sleeping during the five days since you came to Le Lavendou? Your name's not on the register of any of the hotels."

"The other nights could have been just the same as the last, couldn't they?"

And to relight his cigarette, which hadn't gone out, he ostentatiously produced the gold lighter. Of course Battisti noticed it, although he said nothing.

"How long is it since you've seen your Marseille friends? . . . And while you're here, let's have a look at your wallet. . . ."

It contained a fifty-franc note, a bus ticket from Hyères to Toulon, a photograph of a naked woman, and a lock of dark hair.

"Is that all the money you've got left?"

"That's all."

"What are you going to do about it?"

"I've got a job."

"With the old girl?"

"Private secretary."

A handful of people were waiting outside, hoping there'd be an arrest. Little did they imagine that the conversation inside was being conducted in a tone of easy banter, almost of cordiality, Battisti seeming to treat the subject as lightly as Petit Louis himself. But the inspector's voice grew a shade graver when he finally said:

"I'd like to give you a word of advice. . . . Up to now there's not been much harm done. What was your first conviction for?"

"Insulting language to a policeman and assault."

"And the second?"

"I got pinched in a raid on the Modern Bar and they found a gun in my pocket."

"Well, if you take my advice, you won't get caught a third time. Somehow I feel it in my bones that the third time might be very unlucky. You're too sure of yourself. . . . And too fond of showing off."

Petit Louis politely touched his cap, which he hadn't removed, and walked out, pausing for a moment in the doorway to grin at the bystanders.

Half an hour later he was sitting with Constance in a bus. On getting up that morning, he had suggested:

"Suppose we go back to Nice."

Then, with a sidelong look, he had asked:

"You haven't got a car, have you?"

"I used to have one. . . . But it meant keeping a chauffeur. . . ."

Understood! And noted! They'd come back to the question later. Meanwhile, they had to pack into the bus with a crowd of foreigners, who gazed out the windows and went into ecstasies over everything they saw.

It was hot. The air was full of dust and the smell of eucalyptus. Jolted by the bus, Constance half shut her eyes, with a smile of beatitude on her face. Now and then she would suddenly come out of her beautiful dream and hastily look around to make sure Petit Louis belonged to the world of reality.

When they got out in Place Masséna, he muttered:

"We'll take a taxi. . . ."

But Constance demurred.

"It's just around the corner."

He didn't think anything of it at the moment. But when he found himself walking along the street with a heavy suitcase in one hand and an absurd hatbox in the other, he began to feel resentful.

I wonder if she's a miser . . . he reflected.

It was impossible to form any opinion until he saw where she lived. It certainly wasn't far. Crossing the Cours Albert-Premier, they started along Rue de France, took the first turn on the right, a quiet street with big yellow houses on either side, all built alike.

"I hope I didn't pack my key in the suitcase," she panted, because he had made her walk fast. "I'm always doing something silly. . . ."

He didn't answer, merely giving her a dirty look. Fortunately, she didn't see it, or it would have marred her happiness. And she was radiantly happy. She looked up at the windows on either side, hoping there would be someone to see her return home with her conquest.

"Here we are! . . . Wait a moment."

A marble plaque was engraved VILLA CARNOT, and it was obvious at a glance that it was divided up into apartments. On a board in the hall were the names of at least thirty tenants, among whom were a midwife, two doctors, one with a Russian name, a masseuse, and a singing teacher.

The stairs were of marble, too. Constance led the way up to the third floor, where she turned to the left into a hallway where the marbling was only imitation. Stopping in front of a door, she started fumbling for her key.

Another door opened, the one of the next apartment, and Petit Louis saw a girl scantily covered by a dressing gown. Her hair was tousled, her eyes, as she looked at him, somber.

"Who's that?" he asked when they were inside.

"A girl. And she's no good either. . . . Some sort of a gypsy, I would say. . . . Petit Louis! . . .

"What?"

"I hope you're not going to start running after the neighbors, at least."

She tried to say it jokingly, but he could feel the jealousy welling up in her. Calmly, he put down the suitcase and the hatbox, and walked over to throw open the shutters, saying:

"There's one thing we'd better get straight at once, Constance. What I do's my business, and I won't have you questioning it!"

"There! You've said it again!"

"All right, Coco, if you like it better."

"You're being wicked!"

No! He wasn't going to soften. He didn't want any tears or any of those long-drawn-out slobbery kisses she liked to smother him with.

He had more serious things to think about. He looked around critically, wondering whether to be pleased with the place or not.

"Is this the living room?"

"There are only three rooms and the hall. . . . But if Niuta went, we could have her rooms, too."

"The girl next door?"

"Yes . . . I'm afraid the place is in a dreadful mess. But when I left, I had no idea I'd be bringing someone back with me."

She was scared to death he might get a bad impression. She fussed around, putting an ornament back in its place, patting a cushion.

"Don't go into my room yet. I'll have a look first."

It wasn't too bad. Though it wasn't too good either. It was like the rest of the house, like her name itself, typical of the Nice of 1900, with lots of plush and complicated bronzes, dark upholstery and dark hangings, ornaments of mother-of-pearl and spun glass.

In the place of honor above the mantelpiece was an enlarged photograph of a square-faced man with gray hair. In his buttonhole was the ribbon of the Legion of Honor.

"You can come in. . . . Tomorrow I'll have the whole place cleaned up."

An ornate room, but quite pleasant in its oversweet way. Blue satin predominated. In the middle stood Constance, who had found time to change into a negligee.

"Do you pay a lot?" asked Petit Louis.

"Six hundred francs a month, plus the extras."

"And the other room?"

"I'll have to see to that. I've been using it as a storage room."

It was a small bedroom, intended, no doubt, for a maid, since it faced a court and was furnished with an iron bed, a rickety washstand, and a narrow wardrobe. The rest of the space was filled with trunks and boxes, surplus chairs, pictures, photographs, and junk of all sorts.

"We'll soon change it," she rattled on. "With a little taste, we'll make a cozy little den for you."

He didn't say yes, and he didn't say no. He was thinking it over, weighing it. Finally, he asked:

"Isn't there a kitchen?"

"A tiny one."

She showed it to him: a sort of closet with a little gas stove and a few blackened pots and pans.

"Who's the fellow in the living room?"

"Who?"

"You know who I mean. . . . The man in the photograph."

"I'd better explain. . . ."

Petit Louis had taken off his jacket and was continuing his inspection in his shirt sleeves.

"Are you listening?"

"Of course I am."

"I told you I'd been married. . . . That was quite true. I was barely seventeen at the time."

Petit Louis was opening drawers and cabinets to see what was in them. A lot he cared about her marriage at seventeen! She could have been married six times for all he cared.

"After that, I got to know a man who couldn't get a divorce, because he was in a very high position. So I became his mistress. . . . That's when I came to live in Nice. I had a fine villa and a car and a manservant. . . . What did you say?"

"Me? . . . Nothing."

"Then he died. . . ."

If only Petit Louis would keep still for a minute. He was on the go all the time, wandering into the other room, then back again.

"And one of his friends . . ."

"Cut it short! . . . How many have you had?"

"Three . . . Distinguished men, all of them. And highly placed . . . The present one's in the diplomatic service. . . ."

"Does he come often?"

"Twice a month . . . The first and third Fridays . . ."

"Does he sleep here?"

"Yes," she admitted, blushing.

"And the housework?"

"What about it?"

"Who does it?"

She seemed taken aback, and he was sure she was going to lie.

"I sent my maid away some time ago, when I caught her pinching things. . . . I really haven't had time to look for another. . . . Meanwhile, the concierge lends me a hand in the morning."

So! He understood. He could picture her in the morning bustling about in a cloud of dust with her hair tied up in a kerchief and her feet in slippers.

"Do you have your meals here?"

"In the middle of the day . . . In the evening, I go out. There's a little restaurant on the corner, where practically nobody ever goes except regular customers, and they're very nice people, many of them Russians."

Suddenly Petit Louis picked up his jacket, which he'd thrown on the bed. Putting it over his arm, he grunted:

"So long!"

"Are you going out?"

"It'll give you time to get my room ready."

"But you'll come back, won't you?"

He shrugged his shoulders. Of course he'd come back! He allowed her to escort him to the landing, and even accepted a wet kiss on his cheek, while he threw a glance at Niuta's door. Then he went downstairs whistling.

He carefully read all the names on the board in the hall. When he found himself in the street, he looked for the nearest bar, where he discreetly gathered a certain amount of information.

Twenty minutes later, he was sitting at a table on the terrace of a bar painted sky blue, writing painfully with a bad pen that scratched and spluttered over the paper.

My dear Lulu,

Don't be surprised I'm writing from Nice and I'm not here for what you might think so don't think it. The thing is I've met a dame a good class one who's offered me a room in her apartment.

When I say good class don't misunderstand me. First of all she said her name was Constance d'Orval, but when I went through her papers when she wasn't looking I found she was really called Constance Ropiquet. . . . So you see!

We'll see what it brings in. Her head's completely turned and she's all over me but I suspect her of being pretty close when it comes to money.

You'd better go all the same and get some things from my room and send them here. I'll want my other suit and some shirts and socks. Put them in my suitcase and address it to me at the station. I'll call for it.

No news from the gang yet. If you hear anything write me at once *poste restante*. I'll go every day. And send me some money to get along with, because I don't know when they'll be paying up.

I hope Gène hasn't been to see you again. If he does tell him from me that I may make it unpleasant for him.

Remember me to Mme Adèle.

With love.

Having mailed the letter, he went and had a shave and a haircut, leaving the barber's smelling of hair tonic.

The Lavendou affair was in the papers. They said the thieves had got away with about two hundred and ten thousand francs. One of the cars had been found on the Corniche de l'Estérel at Trayas. The other had been discovered by its owner in Toulon within a couple of hundred yards of where it had been stolen.

M. Battisti, the well-known inspector of the flying squad, has interviewed several people, and seems to be on a solid track.

The air was as sweet as candy, and the colors of the town were like bonbons. Petit Louis smiled at the thought of Constance, who was no doubt rushing around with the concierge in a frantic hurry to get his room ready. But it faded away quickly when he thought of the taxi she hadn't wanted to take, and then of the remark she had made about him and the girl opposite.

"Needs some education," he muttered. "I'll have to see to that."

He had been to Nice several times and knew his way around, but he didn't feel at home there as he did in Marseille and Toulon. It was with a mistrustful eye that he looked at the terraces of the cafés, thronged with men in white pants and Panama hats and old ladies of the same breed as Constance. He almost went into the Casino de la Jetée, but remembered in time that he now had only forty francs in his pocket.

It was four o'clock when he left the Villa Carnot. Now it was six. The Promenade des Anglais was seething with people, and a little hydroplane kept taking off and coming down again, making a noise that soon became irritating.

Suppose I telephone Marguerite? he thought.

The truth was that he didn't know what to do with himself. He had to give Constance enough time to get his room ready. And he had to make her think that he had something else to do but sit around with her all day.

Finally he went into a telephone booth and put through a call to the Bar des Amis in La Seyne.

Marguerite was his sister and three years older. She had married the owner of the bar, which did a flourishing business, being situated just outside the naval dockyard.

"Is that you, Marguerite? . . . It's Louis. . . . What's that? . . . No. From Nice. . . . I'll tell you all about it later. . . . Is Fernand there? . . . Tell him everything's all right. . . . Yes, Battisti tried it on but I didn't let him get away with it. . . . Hello! . . . Listen . . . If you see the others . . . You know what I mean? . . . I don't want to be had. . . . That's all. So long, Rite. . . ."

They seemed nothing, those few kilometers he had done in the bus, but they might as well have transported him to another country. He felt altogether out of his element. In Toulon there were fifty bars where everybody knew him and would shake his hand. In Marseille he couldn't be out for five minutes without running into someone he knew. And in all the little country places around, so long as there was a bar and some men to play bowls with, he felt perfectly at home.

To pass the time, he went to a movie. After that he had some ravioli, and at eleven o'clock he was sauntering all alone down Avenue de la Victoire. With his hand in his pocket, he fondled the gold lighter. A little jeweler's shop was still open, for the benefit of unlucky gamblers. Catching sight of it, he was unable to resist the temptation to go in.

"How much is it worth?" he asked.

The middle-aged Jewess behind the counter looked him up and down.

"Do you want to sell it?"

"If you give me a decent price."

"Have you got your identity card?"

He smiled, for he had read her thoughts.

"You needn't worry. I haven't stolen it."

"I didn't say anything about stealing."

"Even if you had, I wouldn't take offense! . . . How much?"

"I can't give you more than three hundred francs."

"Which means it's worth a thousand?"

"It might have been when it was bought. But secondhand . . ."

"All right. Fork over."

"I can't do that. Leave me your address, and I'll send you the money. That's the law. . . ."

He hesitated, then made up his mind.

"Nothing doing!"

If she'd given him the cash, he'd have sold it. But if he had to wait . . .

The strange thing was that every quarter of an hour, at least, his thoughts kept reverting to the little dark girl he'd caught a glimpse of, who lived in the next apartment. He'd have a closer look at her one of these days.

He wasn't in the least anxious to go home, but there seemed no alternative. He'd had enough of wandering around at loose ends. As soon as he reached the third floor, he spotted Constance, who was waiting for him behind the half-open door.

"Quick! Come in. I was beginning to think I'd never see you again. . . . What have you been doing all this time?"

She had on a purple dressing gown fringed with little white feathers, which managed to make her look vaguely like a bishop.

"Have you had anything to eat?"

"Of course."

"And I had prepared . . ."

She had prepared, yes! The room was lighted softly by shaded lamps. On a little table was a cold chicken with some salad, half a crayfish, and a bottle of cassis wine.

"You're sure you're not hungry?"

She smiled, still hoping for some sign of gratitude or tenderness in him. But, though there was no particular reason for it, he was in a surly mood, and for answer he merely asked:

"What does he do, exactly?"

"Who?"

"Your old fellow . . . The photo . . ."

"I told you he was in the diplomatic service."

That sounded pretty vague. He would have liked some details. But he had already pushed open the door of his room, which had been completely cleaned out and rearranged, with a vase of flowers on the table.

"I'm sleepy." He yawned, standing in the doorway.

"Already?"

"By the way, you'll have to give me a key."

"I'll get one made."

"That's the idea. . . . Good night . . ."

He turned around, hesitated, then on an impulse asked:

"What did that lighter cost?"

"I don't know. It was given to me."

"Who by? . . . The photo? . . ."

"As a matter of fact . . ."

"Was it given to you or did you buy it?"

"I bought it. One day when I'd won at the casino."

"Do you gamble?"

"A little . . . well, nearly every evening."

"How much?"

"How much what?"

"Did you pay for the lighter?"

"Fourteen hundred francs. It was fifteen hundred, but I beat them down."

Then, abruptly, he broke off the conversation with a curt:

"Good night!"

And without looking at her, he shut the door, sat down on the edge of the bed, and took off his shoes.

He knew perfectly well that she was standing on the other side of the door, listening for the slightest sound, hoping he would relent. But there were too many things jarring on his nerves. He didn't feel like softening. Sulkily, he got in bed and switched off the light. Lying with his eyes open, he could see the shadow of two fat legs in the crack of light under the door.

3

AT FIRST SIGHT, Petit Louis looked his usual self as he got out of the bus in Place du Marché in Hyères. His white cap, nicely flattened on his head, his pointed shoes, the nonchalance of his gait, his way of looking at people as an actor surveys the anonymous crowd applauding him—it was Petit Louis all over.

Sitting at a table in front of a brasserie were two bearded men whose faces were vaguely familiar. He gave them a casual wave of the hand as he went by, making for Rue du Rempart.

It was two in the afternoon. There was no shade on either side of the steep stony street, and Petit Louis, who hated nothing more than perspiring, had to stop every other minute to cool off.

The farther he went, the fewer people he met, and little by little his expression changed, becoming hard, mistrustful, and even slightly anxious.

First of all, why had Louise let a whole week go by without answering his letter? And then, why hadn't the expected advertisement appeared in the *Petit Marseillais*?

Brace of pigeons for sale. Fine birds. Write . . .

Finally, he'd phoned Louise one morning at a time he'd be sure to find her, because she'd still be asleep. He'd had to wait a long time, and when she came to the phone, he'd hardly recognized her voice.

"Is that you? . . . Don't say anything rash. . . . I'll write. . . ."

That was all she could find to say to him. When her letter finally arrived it said:

> Gène's been here and he's not at all pleased. He told me to tell you to lie low until further orders. You mustn't come here. . . .

By now Rue du Rempart was totally deserted. In a workshop with a blue-washed skylight, a carpenter was planing; after that came a large house with closed shutters, standing at the corner of a cross street.

It was right at the outskirts of town. The little gardens were enclosed by old stone walls, and a couple of hundred yards farther on was open country.

When he got to the corner house, Petit Louis found himself in the presence of three women reclining in deck chairs; a fourth was sitting on the doorstep. It was siesta time. Their florid dressing gowns did not conceal their bare thighs or their chemises. A little farther on some children were playing on the same sidewalk.

All four gazed at Petit Louis, and one of them, the one on the doorstep, jumped to her feet, saying:

"Didn't you get my letter?"

He shrugged his shoulders. He gave no greeting to the others, though he knew them. With his hands in his pockets and a cigarette between his lips, he moved toward the door.

"Go inside," he ordered.

And he practically pushed her indoors, into a cool, shady room whose principal piece of furniture was an immense player piano. A little girl of six, the daughter of the manager, was playing with her doll.

"Sit down!"

"What's the matter with you?" asked Louise, astonished, gathering her dressing gown over her sky-blue chemise.

She was dark; her very pale smooth skin had hardly a trace of down on it. She sat at a table, and Petit Louis sat on the other side, opposite her.

"I told you not to come."

"I know."

He didn't smile, didn't try to look pleasant. On the contrary, he looked her straight in the eye, sternly, and he said nothing on purpose, to get her rattled.

He succeeded. She forced a smile to her lips and murmured:

"What's the matter?"

The window beside them was open but the outside shutters were closed, allowing only a cool, filtered light to pass through. The little girl looked up from her doll from time to time to study them.

"I'm waiting for an explanation."

"I told you: Gène came . . ."

"What about it?"

"He's furious. . . ."

A bit of blue chemise was still visible, contrasting with Louise Mazzone's pale, sallow skin. A sweet smell of verbena came from her hair.

"What's bothering him?"

"He says you've played the fool. . . . First of all, in staying behind in Le Lavendou to show off, and then in trying to be clever with Inspector Battisti. . . . He says you're no use for anything except playing to the gallery."

"And what else?"

"That you couldn't even keep your mouth shut. He says you must have talked to someone, because there's no other explanation. . . . The day before yesterday, the police raided the Bar Express and went all over the place with a fine-tooth comb."

The words gave him a stab, but he did his utmost not to wince.

"Battisti said himself that somebody'd tipped them off. And what's more, he said it was the chief croupier at the Casino de la Jetée."

"Did they find anything?"

"No! But they're absolutely furious with you all the same, Gène, Charlie, and the Lyonnais. . . . It's true you always were a chatterbox."

"I'll trouble you to mind your own business," he snapped.

He was more humiliated than angry. He understood what had happened. One evening, when he'd been reading the *Eclaireur de Nice*, he had said to Constance:

"And to think that the swag is hidden in a little bar in the Vieux Port in Marseille!"

He didn't remember having mentioned the bar by name, but he must have, and Constance, who went to the casino nearly every night, had no doubt wanted to show off, too, and had passed it on to the chief croupier.

"If they took the trouble to look in the Vieux Port in Marseille. In a little bar . . ."

And of course it had got to Battisti.

The little girl had come over and was standing a couple of feet from Petit Louis, staring into his face as though he was the most astonishing spectacle in the world.

"Can't you go and play somewhere else?"

And to Louise:

"When are they going to give me my share?"

"That's just it. . . . Not for many a long day . . . There's going to be no division until the police have found something else to take an interest in."

"Look . . ."

"What?"

"Are you sure they're going to give me my share?"

"As a matter of fact . . ."

Outside, the women went on with their siesta, dozing in their deck chairs, while the rare passers-by turned around and grinned.

Then heavy steps were heard on the stairs, and the next moment an enormous woman put her head in the door, calling:

"Odette! . . . Come here at once! . . ."

She sent the child upstairs, then came into the room, looking none too pleased. Ignoring Petit Louis, she said to Louise:

"What did I tell you?"

"But I told him not to come."

"What's all this?" growled Petit Louis. "Don't I have the right to come and see my own girl?"

The woman muttered something between her teeth, which made him flare up.

"Repeat that, will you?" he hissed, seizing her by the shoulder. "Repeat it! . . . Or maybe you'd rather not!"

"All right! . . . I said it's not so certain that she *is* your girl."

"What do you mean?"

"Anyway, it was Gène who placed her here, and, because I don't want any trouble . . . Take your hands off me, young man. . . . That's not the way to behave with a woman like me. . . . It won't be many minutes before the customers start coming, and I'd like you out of the way by then. . . ."

"What did she mean?" he asked a moment later, thrusting his face into Louise's.

"I don't know. . . ."

"You're lying! . . . What did she mean, saying that about Gène? Is it true? . . ."

"I was Gène's girl first. . . ."

"And now?"

He had understood. Gène still thought he had rights over her. Besides, Gène had never taken him seriously, and, in derision, persisted in referring to him as "the Artist."

"Get dressed," he ordered, "and pack your things."

"But . . ."

"Listen! . . . I've got some patience, but not a hell of a lot. If you don't join me outside five minutes from now, I'll come back and do something you'll all be sorry for. . . . Is that clear?"

He went out and walked off, without so much as a glance at the women sprawling on the sidewalk. When he'd gone a hundred yards, however, he stopped and waited, leaning against a wall.

He didn't count the minutes. He was wise not to; for it was nearly a quarter of an hour before a door opened and Louise emerged furtively, with an anxious look on her face. She was dressed in a brown coat and skirt, and was carrying a small fiber suitcase.

She trotted toward him, looking back over her shoulder every ten steps, then slipped her arm through his. After a minute's silence she said resentfully:

"I think you're being very rash...."

In the bus they didn't exchange a single word. At Nice, they got off on Avenue de la Californie, and Petit Louis, without breaking the silence between them, chose a little three-story hotel and took a room by the week.

It had no running water. The bedspread was of thick gray cotton, the washstand of bamboo.

"I know what I'm doing," he said at last. "Gène may think himself very smart, but I'm not going to have him thinking he can teach me a lesson...."

The window was open. Outside, the night was still and wet. They could hear cars slithering by.

"Besides, I never liked the idea of your being in *that* house."

Perhaps the long hours in the bus had softened him. In any case, he seemed touched, almost tender.

"What are you waiting for? Why don't you take your things off? . . . Aren't you pleased that I got you away from there?"

"I'm wondering what's going to happen."

He began talking. He had rarely talked so much in his life before. Every few minutes he went and looked out the window at the festoons of light, as though deliberately to stimulate his excitement.

"You'll see. I can work as fast as any of them. . . . Here! Take this to get along with. . . ."

And from one of his pockets he produced a ring. It was one of those family rings of no great value—a garnet surrounded by tiny lusterless pearls.

"She gave it to me yesterday. She gives me anything I want. . . . Among her papers I found a receipt for a mink coat, which she put in storage for the summer. . . ."

"Who is she?"

"As I told you, her name's not really d'Orval at all. According to her papers, she's Madame Ropiquet, widow. Her maiden name was Salmon. . . . All I really know about her is that she doesn't have to work, and that she writes quite a lot of letters to a lawyer in Orléans."

"What about?"

"Don't know. . . . Tomorrow, or the day after, you must go to the casino. We'll meet you as if by accident, and I'll introduce you as a relative."

Louise was not enthusiastic, but she resigned herself. To fill in the time, she unpacked the few clothes she'd brought with her and remade the bed to her own liking.

"Yesterday I gave her a good hiding, for the first time. . . . I was outside in the hall, spinning a yarn to the girl next door, a Rumanian who always manages to open her door when I'm passing. Then Constance came out and started making a scene."

"How did she take it?"

"What?"

"The beating."

"She apologized. Begged me not to leave her. Swore she'd kill herself if I did. . . . Come on, let's go out. It's not midnight yet."

They walked together along the Promenade des Anglais, Louise, as before, hanging on his arm. Petit Louis kept his hands in his pockets, and he walked with a long stride on purpose, to emphasize the difference between them.

For long periods they walked in silence, meeting people whose faces were hardly visible in the dim light. They stared at the luxury hotels, brightly lighted, and at the equally luxurious limousines that drew up in front of them. Then, abruptly, Petit Louis would make a remark or two.

"They're fools. . . ."

"Who?"

"Gène. The whole bunch of them."

It had got right under his skin, and he only worked it out bit by bit in occasional outbursts.

"They'll always go on doing the same thing in exactly the same way. . . . They haven't got an ounce of brains among them. . . . The Lyonnais, I admit, has had some experience, but he thinks too much of himself. . . ."

"Suppose we run into her? . . . The old woman . . ."

"Not a chance. At this time of night she's at the Casino de la Jetée, timidly staking a five-franc piece. . . . I'm afraid she's a miser."

But his thoughts soon reverted to Gène, Charlie, and the Lyonnais. Others, too. Titin, for instance, and all the gang that were known as the "Marseillais," among whom he was never taken seriously.

"You should have stuck to being a cabinetmaker," they often told him.

For he had learned a trade, a real one. When the German armies had advanced in 1914, his mother had fled from Lille, and had ended up, Heaven knows why, in the little village of Le Farlet, between Toulon and Carqueiranne.

A widow with two small children, she had been a charwoman until an old man named Dutto, a wine grower on a big scale, took her into his house as a servant, and as everything else, for that matter, according to local gossip.

Petit Louis had started his apprenticeship with a joiner in Le Farlet. Then one day he had gone off to Toulon, and then, from one place to another, he had worked his way to Lyon.

Up to the time of his military service, he had worked fairly regularly. And even afterward he had returned to his trade from time to time, at Marseille, at Saint-Tropez, six months at Sète, and then once more in Toulon.

"You should have stuck to it," sneered the gang in Marseille.

And later, when he had a girl in that house, and when he gave them a hand now and then, they persisted in calling him "the Artist."

"If they don't cough up, I'll damn well make 'em . . ." he threatened suddenly, as they passed the casino.

Then an idea struck him.

"Would you like to see her? . . . Look! . . . I'll go in first, and when you come in I'll be standing behind her."

"I'm not dressed."

"That doesn't matter. . . . Have you got any money? You have to get a ticket to play."

He walked in like an old regular and wandered around the tables, almost immediately catching sight of Constance Ropiquet, playing roulette at the far end of the room. She was sitting next to the croupier, as she always did.

She always had a seat, no matter how long she had to wait for it, and always on the left of the croupier. Once settled down, she took out a little silver pencil, a hundred-franc note, and some roulette cards, on which she noted every coup.

A minute later, Louise appeared, and Petit Louis gave her an almost imperceptible smile and went and stood behind Constance, who jumped when she suddenly realized he was there.

"Hush!" she whispered, putting a finger to her lips and pointing to the imposing pile of counters in front of her. "Go and wait for me in the bar."

Then, with a maternal gesture, she shoved a handful of counters into his hand and turned toward the croupier.

"Am I too late?"

"You'd better be quick. . . . Nothing more . . . The seven . . ."

Constance looked back at Petit Louis, pointed to the seven

and the fresh winnings that were pushed toward her. Her eyes swam with joy and pride.

"Does she often win?"

They were sitting in the bar, and Louise, who was always hungry at midnight because of her irregular hours, had ordered a sandwich. From their high stools, they could survey the whole playing room. There were few people in evening dress, but plenty of middle-aged women like Constance Ropiquet.

"Make your bets. . . . Nothing more . . ."

"Does she often win?" asked Louise again.

"Sometimes . . . But since she never stakes more than five francs at a time . . ."

"You don't know where her money comes from?"

"I know one source—an old man who comes to see her twice a month. She swears he's something high up. A diplomat . . . I haven't seen him yet."

"Won't she be jealous when she sees me?"

"Not when I tell her you're my sister."

To which Louise merely remarked:

"That's a pretty tiepin you're wearing."

Sitting there with her beside him, Petit Louis already felt a lot better. There was no doubt about it: he had scored a point against Gène.

"I've got to go easy with her, you know. No use trying to rush things. First of all, I must find out just what she's got. It shouldn't be difficult. She's bone lazy and has already got me to write two letters for her. Only, they weren't interesting ones . . ."

"Look out!" said Louise, hiding her mouth behind her sandwich.

Constance approached, obviously taken aback. Petit Louis, however, pretended not to notice it, and turning toward her said:

"This is my sister, Louise. . . . My friend Madame Constance d'Orval . . ."

34

"Charmed, Madame . . ."

"My sister arrived this evening. She's staying a few days."

"Are you staying in a hotel?" asked Constance, in her best society voice.

"No," interposed Petit Louis. "Some friends are putting her up. . . . She has a lot of friends along the coast. Her husband was from Nice. . . ."

"Oh? You're married?"

Petit Louis couldn't prevent his eyes from sparkling with glee, but he thought he'd better cut the scene short.

"Let's go and have a drink somewhere."

He glanced at Constance's hands. She understood his look and pitifully confessed:

"I lost it all. The seven turned up three times running, and I felt sure it would go on."

Near the door, the chief croupier was studying them with cold, professional indifference. On a seat in a corner, a police inspector was waiting patiently for the night's play to draw to a close.

Louise Mazzone tried to be amiable, but every now and then a scared look came into her eyes, when she thought that they must already have telephoned to Gène at the Bar Express, and she wondered what he'd do. She even calculated how long it would take him to come from Marseille by train.

"That girl's here," whispered Constance to Petit Louis.

"What girl?"

"Our neighbor. It's positively scandalous. She has no right to run after a man like that. She's not even reached the age of consent."

She was referring to Niuta, who had entered accompanied by a young man. She took no notice of Petit Louis.

The entrance hall was deserted, the showcases dark. Outside, a row of taxis waited to take players home. Beyond, the regular sighing of the sea was interrupted occasionally by the cry of a sea gull.

"Where are we going?" asked Constance.

"La Californie . . . " suggested Petit Louis, who wasn't at all ready for bed.

They squeezed into a taxi. His knee touched Louise's, and Constance held his hand. They went, in succession, to three third-rate nightclubs, where the women drank champagne and Petit Louis *menthe verte*. Constance and Louise seemed to be getting on together easily.

"Do you live in Paris?"

"Part of the year . . ."

"When my husband was alive . . ."

At four in the morning, they were having an argument in Place Masséna.

"But I tell you it's no trouble at all," said Constance. "That's right, Louise, isn't it? It's absurd to go and wake up your friends at this hour of the morning. I can lend you a nightgown, and you can sleep with me."

Louise and Petit Louis had trouble keeping a straight face.

Constance was all over them. She insisted in making coffee, in which she put a lavish dash of brandy.

"I can lend you a dressing gown. You go into the other room, Louis, while your sister undresses."

They sat up a long time chatting in the room with the soft cushions and faded hangings, while the last lonely taxis wandered through the street below.

4

IT WAS VERY NEARLY bliss, at any rate as Petit Louis had imagined it when he'd worked as a cabinetmaker and when he'd gazed enviously at another race of mortals, the Marseillais, who, with clean hands and well-polished pointed shoes, could spend their days sitting at little tables outside bars.

Now his hands were clean, too, and without his having used a pumice stone. And the day before, he had even—for the first time in his life—had a manicure, at the smartest hairdresser's in the Cours Albert-Premier.

With his eyes half shut, he studied his square fingers and his nails, which had been lacquered pink, while at the same time he listened to the sounds in the house.

It wasn't merely laziness that kept him in bed till noon. He did it also on principle—to get back at those many mornings when, before daybreak, a shrill alarm clock had drilled its way through his sleep.

The morning papers were lying by his side. Constance had brought them in with his black coffee. She had lit his first cigarette, and had opened the outside shutters just sufficiently to allow a beam of light to reach the bed, a narrow, slanting beam such as one sees in pictures of the Annunciation.

Louise, in a dressing gown, was no doubt dusting the living room. It was really very funny. And still funnier to think that she was there by Constance's express invitation.

"Why should you go and stay with friends when there's room for you here with your brother?"

The first night, they had slept in the same bed, and next morning Louise had whispered to Petit Louis:

"There's a musty smell about that old girl. . . . I don't know how you can put up with her."

Then a couch had been installed in a corner of the living room, and now Louise was part of the household, so much so that nobody seemed to remember when she'd arrived, and there had been no further talk of her departure.

The fact that she was patient and good-tempered had a lot to do with it. A sweet nature, said Constance, who found her a docile listener to her interminable prattle as they sat together by the window with their crocheting or their knitting. From time to time, the girl would gravely put in a word of approval, such as:

"How true!"

Or:

"I quite understand."

In the mornings, their hair tied up in kerchiefs, they both did the housework. Soon one of them would go out to do the shopping. They took turns.

When it was Louise's turn, Constance would rush straight in to Petit Louis, brimming over with delight, and say, with a meaningful look:

"Louise has gone out. . . ."

The other days, it was Louise, who came in calmly, and more often than not she would merely sit on the edge of the bed chatting quietly.

There were other sounds, besides those of the housework, that came to Petit Louis's ears. There were those from the street, which, in the morning, always had a certain piquant freshness. There were those from inside the house, and one in particular for which he waited with ever-increasing impatience. That was Niuta's voice, in the room on the other side of the lath-and-plaster wall.

She studied singing. He'd learned that from the concierge. She wasn't really a Rumanian. It was all rather complicated. Her mother was a famous singer, who now lived in America; her father was supposed to be a Russian.

She was only sixteen and a half, but her parents couldn't be bothered with her. To get her out of the way, she had been sent to Nice, where a monthly allowance was paid to her by one of the banks.

Petit Louis was convinced she was wildly in love with him. She must have been constantly on the watch for him, because she invariably managed to open her door just as he was going out.

Yet the only time he'd tried to enter her apartment—in his best cocksure manner—she had darted back into her bedroom and double-locked the door.

Ever since then Petit Louis had had her on his mind, and in the morning he would put down his newspaper to listen to her singing.

He was thoroughly pleased with life, there was no doubt about that. Naturally, he'd have been better pleased still if Niuta had been in bed beside him. But he felt sure it would happen one of these days. It was just a matter of time. He'd scared her by going too fast, forgetting that she was only a child. Since then, he had merely smiled at her, with the gay, childlike, disarming smile that he could summon at will.

Yes, he was happy. And what could prove it more conclusively than that vague, almost physical apprehension that wormed its way into his consciousness? It was only logical. You can never be really happy without occasionally feeling a little pang of dread lest it escape you. . . .

He hadn't run into Gène, or any of the others. Neither had he had any direct news of them. But Louise had had a letter saying that, as a result of her departure, the manager had taken a trip to Marseille. And that might mean a lot of things.

Someone was using a typewriter on the floor above. It happened every morning from nine o'clock on. It was an elderly woman, the widow of a civil servant, who worked at home typing manuscripts.

Petit Louis had made inquiries about every occupant of the house, in the first place from curiosity, but also because you never knew what information might be useful.

It must have been about eleven o'clock. The doorbell rang, which was unusual, because regular callers, like the men who read the meters and the deliverymen, knew that the door wasn't locked and came right in, calling out:

"M'ame Constance!"

Without moving, with his head on the pillow and a cigarette between his lips, Petit Louis pricked up his ears. He heard a man's voice, but it wasn't until Louise came into the room that he knew who it was. She looked worried, made a sign to him to keep quiet, and whispered:

"It's a police inspector."

"Which one?"

"I don't know. He sent me away."

Petit Louis got up at once and stood barefoot in his striped silk pajamas with his ear close to a panel of the door. Louise put her head close to his and listened, too.

"Will you take a seat?" they heard Constance say. "Excuse my not being dressed, but at this time of day I'm always busy with the housework."

And at this time of day, her eyes were puffy and her cheeks pasty.

"Can you tell me if this is yours?" asked the inspector, holding out something that Petit Louis couldn't see.

"Yes. It's mine. . . . It was left to me by my poor mother. . . .

But how did you get hold of it? Did someone find it in the street?"

"Unfortunately not. This gold cross was sold the day before yesterday to a jeweler on Avenue de la Victoire. . . . The thief . . ."

Constance uttered a little cry. Behind the door, Petit Louis stood gazing at Louise's frowning eyebrows.

"What makes you say the thief?" asked Constance in an unsteady voice.

"Because I assumed it was stolen from you."

"But suppose I gave it to someone?"

"Who?"

"Suppose I asked my secretary, Louis Bert, to sell it for me?"

"Did you ask him to sell this ring, too?"

"Certainly . . . I've had enough of these old-fashioned jewels, so I asked him to get rid of them for me."

Petit Louis winked, and Louise's frown began to relax.

"In that case, I've nothing to say. . . . If that's your attitude . . ."

"Well . . ."

"Still, I've been instructed to give you certain information. . . . Are you aware that this Petit Louis, whom you call your secretary, has been in prison twice?"

"Yes. He told me so. . . ."

"Do you know that he stands a very good chance of going there again for the raid on the post office in Le Lavendou?"

"How do you know it was he?"

Good old Constance! Petit Louis couldn't help smiling. He felt like suddenly throwing open the door and ironically saluting that fool of an inspector.

"Well . . . It's your business. . . . You've got him in your house, and it's for you to decide whether he stays. If you're wise . . . But, never mind! . . . My duty is simply to let you know the facts, so that, if anything happens, it won't be our fault."

This time, Petit Louis shrugged his shoulders; then, like a schoolboy, he did some shadowboxing.

"What do you mean? What can happen to me?"

"You're no longer young. . . . I imagine you to be wealthy enough to be an attractive prey to a young man with no means of support. . . ."

"Really!" protested Constance, drawing herself up with dignity. "Really! I beg you . . ."

"All right! There's no need to get angry. . . . One last question: did Petit Louis tell you who the girl is who's living under your roof? The girl I saw just now? . . .

"She's his sister."

The jaunty look vanished from Petit Louis's face. Holding his breath, he listened tensely, while Louise, with a sigh, whispered:

"I told you so!"

The inspector went on complacently, conscious that he had at last got the upper hand:

"I'm sorry to contradict you, but it's my duty to tell you that the person in question is Louise Mazzone, born in Avignon in 1912, and that she came under police supervision in 1932 as a prostitute. When she came here ten days ago, she came from a brothel in Hyères, where she was placed by Petit Louis, who has been living on her earnings. . . . That's all. . . . I'll only add that, if you need any assistance or further information, the police are at your disposal. . . . You can get in touch with me at the Sûreté Nationale."

A silence. A silence all the more impressive because it was impossible to guess what was happening in the next room. At last a door opened and shut, and steps could be heard on the stairs.

Petit Louis and Louise looked at each other sheepishly. Then Petit Louis deliberately assumed once more his jaunty air, scratched the back of his head, and made a silly face.

"What are you going to do?" she whispered.

First of all, he tiptoed over to the looking glass and combed his hair; then he lit a cigarette. Listening at the door again, he thought he could hear the sound of muffled sobs. He sighed, turned the handle, and opened the door.

It was a minute or two before he caught sight of Constance in the bedroom. She had collapsed on the unmade bed in such a shapeless heap that he could only recognize her by the piece of feather-edged dressing gown that was showing.

Collapsed was the word. Completely crushed, she lay face down, all mixed up with the eiderdown, sheets, and blankets, the whole heap heaving in a regular rhythm broken occasionally by a stronger spasm.

"Oooh! . . . Ooh! . . . Ooh! . . ." she whined, in such a strange voice that you'd never have thought it belonged to a stout woman of fifty.

Petit Louis edged around the bed awkwardly, as inexperienced people sometimes do when visiting a sickbed and wondering how to start a conversation.

"Ooh! . . . Ooh! . . ."

Did she know he was there? Had she heard him come into the room? She went on weeping with desperate regularity. There seemed no hope of it stopping. The only part of her he could see was not the prettiest—her fat white legs, striated by blue varicose veins.

"Ooh! . . ."

The two windows were wide open. At one of the windows of the house opposite was a helpless old man, who sat there smoking his pipe, staring into the room with such a fixed expression that he looked like a waxwork.

"Oooh! . . ."

Petit Louis opened his mouth, but shut it again. The draft from the window wafted the smoke of his cigarette across the bed, and she must have smelled it. All at once, instead of the perpetual "Oooh!" she said, but with the same plaintive note:

"Wicked boy!"

And the sound of the words set her off to crying harder than ever.

Petit Louis sat down on the edge of the bed. The fact that she wasn't looking at him made his job much easier, since he didn't have to worry about the expression on his face. Gently, he placed a hand on her shoulder. Then, after a little cough, he said very quietly:

"I heard everything. . . . I was on the other side of the door. . . . I knew it was bound to happen sooner or later."

Silence. Constance went on weeping, but without making any noise, because she didn't want to miss anything he said.

"First of all, if I've been in prison, it wasn't for anything dishonorable. Anybody, in a roughhouse, can sock somebody on the jaw, or kick a policeman on the shin when he's threatening you. . . ."

That wasn't what interested her, he knew very well. But he began that way to give himself time to get worked up for the critical part.

"There's the Lavendou business, I know. . . . But that was only robbing the government, which does no harm to anybody. . . ."

She moved a little, impatient, no doubt, for him to come to the point.

"As for Louise . . . It's easy for people to talk, but they'd do better to ask where these girls come from and how it is they come to that business. . . . Louise's mother had seven children and she was well known for going with anyone who'd pay her a few francs. . . ."

For a moment his mind wandered, as Niuta started singing Chopin's "Berceuse." She sang it every morning, presumably for his benefit, and it never failed in its effect, and that was to excite him.

"When I first met Louise, she was already in a house in Marseille. . . . I tried to get her away, but she was in the hands of someone else, a fellow named Gène, and all I could do . . ."

He was suddenly conscious of an eye, a solitary eye, watching him, an eye that was already dry.

"I managed to get her transferred to Hyères, and then, when I had a little money—thanks to you, of course—I got her away."

44

That eye made everything more difficult. Petit Louis had to arrange the expression on his face to suit his words. And the old man opposite was still staring with his face of wax.

"When I told you she was my sister, it wasn't altogether a lie. For that just about describes our relationship. . . ."

A plaintive voice emerged again from the heap on the bed.

"You've never . . . ?"

"I won't say that. . . . In the beginning, yes. But that's three years ago, when I went to the Marseille place as a customer. . . . And it wasn't long before it was just all over between us—as far as that sort of thing's concerned. . . ."

"Just about!"

"We know each other too well."

The voice was less plaintive now. It was clearer and more insidious.

"You haven't done anything here, in my house? . . . Never? . . ."

"Never!"

"When I go out shopping in the morning?"

She moved again, and a head was raised from the shapeless mass. Then the whole body resumed its normal shape as she slowly lifted herself up and sat on the edge of the bed. There she sat, with one cheek wet, her features swollen, her hair tousled.

"You wouldn't have done that, would you?"

"No. I swear we've never been in bed together since we came here."

"You've never kissed her? On her mouth, I mean."

She spoke in such a tragic voice that Petit Louis found it hard to keep a straight face.

"Not on her mouth, no."

"No cuddling at all?"

"You silly old thing! . . . I've told you—no."

There was only one thing to do now. Never mind! He had to see it through. He leaned over her and took her in his arms, and put his cheek against hers. Like that, she couldn't see his face, and he started talking, in the low, slightly broken voice he knew could work wonders.

"I don't pretend to be a saint, but I'd never do a thing like that. . . . And I'd rather be what I am than what that gentleman is who came just now. . . . It's easy to judge others when you've got everything you need. . . . When I was a kid everybody called me "the refugee." When there were any old clothes around, they used to say:

" 'Don't throw them away. They're good enough for the little refugee.'

"And I wore the cast-off clothes of every boy in Le Farlet.

"And my mother, at old Dutto's, had all the heavy work to do, until in the end she didn't look like a woman at all."

"Stop," murmured Constance.

But he had no intention of stopping. He was just getting into his stride, and he knew he'd got hold of the right end of the stick. There was also a certain sincerity in his sense of grievance. Niuta's voice and Chopin's music had moved him. If only he could have had *her* beside him, he would have poured out all his troubles. Two unfortunates, they could have mingled their tears with their caresses. How sweet it would have been. . . .

"And whenever he felt like it," Petit Louis went on, "that old brute Dutto would call her into his room and slam the door in my face. . . . As ugly as sin, he was, and is still. An Italian who's been forty years in France and never even learned the language . . . He speaks to nobody and hates everybody, suspecting them of being after his money. . . . One day I found him starting to put his dirty hands on my sister. She was fourteen at the time. . . . I told my mother about it, but when she spoke to him she only got a beating for her pains. . . . Well? . . . What kind of an upbringing do you call that?"

"Hush! . . . Don't think about it any more."

"And what sort of life is it to sweat all day long sawing and planing when any amount of worthless fellows do nothing all day long—and thrive on it! . . . Well, there's the truth for you. . . . I didn't see why I should be any dumber than the others. . . ."

She moved her face away from his, to look at him. Then in a sudden access of tenderness she threw her arms around him.

"Wicked boy!" she said again.

But this time it sounded different.

"Listen, Louise."

"Yes, Madame . . ."

Louise had never been able to call Constance by her Christian name, however much Constance might press her.

"I know everything."

"Yes, Madame."

And Louise, less clever than Petit Louis, hung her head pitifully, like a little servant who is being given notice.

"I know all about your life and Petit Louis's! . . . I know that you've been lovers, but that it's all over now. And you love each other like brother and sister."

"Yes, Madame."

A hint of the odor of her recent embrace still hung about Constance; the bed was damp, and there was a deep hollow in it. She had put her make-up back on. Was she perhaps not averse to displaying her languor and letting its cause be guessed?

"I don't want those nasty men from the police to get the better of you. They're trying to put you in the wrong, both of you."

Perhaps, when all's said and done, it gave her a certain satisfaction to be able henceforth to be a little patronizing toward them. Was she not, more than ever, their benefactress?

She had sent Petit Louis out, but he had got no farther than the landing, hoping Niuta's door would open, more obsessed than ever by the desire to take her into his arms.

"And we three will go on together, just as before. There'll be nothing changed. You needn't protest. I've made up my mind about it. If you left now, it would be as good as saying that you've merely been making fun of me. . . . No. I want you to stay, and I'm convinced you'll never let me regret it. . . . Only for today, I'll let you go. You can spend the night at a hotel, both of you. You see, my friend's coming, the diplomat. . . ."

The typewriter clacked away in the room above. At the window opposite, the old man's pipe must have gone out long ago; he had never moved an eyelid. In a cage, on his left, a canary hopped about from one perch to another.

"Now, if you'll help me finish the rooms . . . Then we'll go and have lunch in a restaurant. My friend doesn't arrive till three. That'll give us time to go and have lunch by the sea at Juan-les-Pins. We'll take a taxi. . . ."

"Can I come in again?" asked Petit Louis, who hadn't had a glimpse of Niuta.

"Yes. Come in, bad boy! . . . Go and change quickly. Get into your best suit. I'm taking you both to lunch in Juan-les-Pins in a taxi. . . ."

An hour later, they went from the house to the sunny sidewalk, dressed from head to foot in their Sunday best, so obviously going somewhere special that a taxi drew up beside them without their having hailed it.

"Juan-les-Pins, please. And you needn't go too quickly. . . . Can we have the top down?"

Constance sat between them. . . . After all, it was wiser.

5

IT WAS IN THE MIDDLE of August—or, to be quite exact, on Friday the 19th—that Petit Louis reached, if one may so describe it, the culminating point of his career.

In spite of the heat, Nice was thronged with people, a variegated crowd of vacationers, very different from the visitors who came in winter and spring. Nothing was lacking to turn the town into a huge fun fair, even down to an airplane that offered enthusiasts a baptism of flying at specially reduced prices.

Petit Louis's wardrobe had been restocked, until it could now be said to match the season.

It was the realization of his dream: at any and every hour of the day he was as clean and trim from head to foot as the workman who, on Sunday morning, leaves the barber's hands and has only to put on his white collar to complete the grand picture.

Constance seemed happy. As far as money was concerned, she was quite generous, though she never gave very much at a time, preferring to dole it out bit by bit in sums rarely larger than a hundred francs.

Louise went out by herself. What else was she to do with herself all day long and every evening? If she wasn't back by one in the morning, it meant she was having a night out. She had to be careful, however, since more than once she had seen the inspector who had come to the Villa Carnot, and she felt sure he was keeping an eye on her.

As for Petit Louis, he never had any difficulty in spotting a policeman in plain clothes, and he never failed to pass one with a sneer. They couldn't touch him. He was straight. An acquaintance he had run into had given him the card of a firm of champagne wholesalers, and Petit Louis made great play with it in the bars, offering, with mock solemnity, to take orders.

But in spite of everything, he was unable to get rid of a certain latent uneasiness, and he sometimes wondered whether it wasn't a presentiment. When he'd had meningitis at the age of eleven, he'd said a month before that he was going to be ill; but of course everybody had laughed at him.

Didn't he have everything he wanted? Perhaps not quite, but very nearly. In one direction, admittedly, he had met with something like a rebuff. He had made a round of the bars on a street near the casino, bars in which the more important people of Nice were accustomed to gather, and where they talked about women or the next election, about the grant of some land concessions or a hand of bridge that had been played the night before.

Of course he hadn't come out openly, saying:

"I'm Petit Louis of Le Farlet. Can you move over a little to make room for me in your circle?"

He went about it more gingerly, hovering around to listen to their conversation or watch their games of cards. Once, he had rather shyly challenged one of them to a throw of dice for a drink.

He hadn't cut any ice. Some of them looked at him with curiosity, others with indifference or even contempt. No one seemed inclined to give him a chance.

Giving up, he had looked for consolation in bars of a different stamp, where he knew he could be somebody, bars frequented by young people, some of good family, who were ready to accept anything that harmonized with their idea of emancipation.

An uneasiness, certainly, but one that wasn't formulated. Or, if it was, it would take shape in the prospect of suddenly finding himself face to face with Gène, or Charlie, or any of the Marseille gang. He knew, however, that they were never eager to come to Nice. It wasn't their territory, and they were apt to get an unpleasant welcome from those whose preserve it was.

The great evening with Monsieur Parpin—the one on Friday, August 19—began, like so many incidents in Petit Louis's life, with a chance remark intended merely as a joke.

Monsieur Parpin was Constance's friend. And, just as she was not really Constance d'Orval at all, but Constance Ropiquet, so he, the diplomat, was not really a diplomat, but a retired chief customs inspector from some town in the North. Petit Louis had taken the trouble to find out all about him. He had two married daughters, one in Nice, the other, with whom he lived, in Arles.

He came regularly to see his daughter in Nice, taking the opportunity to spend a night with Constance, whose acquaintance he had made on the Promenade des Anglais. He was seventy-two, and invariably carried a silk umbrella, which in summer did duty as a parasol.

On that Friday morning, Constance sighed, and said:

"Pépé's due today. There's another evening spoiled."

She called him Pépé, Heaven knows why. Apparently she didn't realize how ridiculous it sounded.

After a moment's reflection, she added:

"I wonder if he'll remember it's my birthday."

For Pépé was just the man for presents. He was full of little attentions, and never went anywhere empty-handed. A grandfather, he no doubt spoiled his grandchildren in much the same fond way as he did Constance.

"It's your birthday, is it?" asked Petit Louis. "And how many have you had already?"

"Don't be nasty!"

"Look! Why shouldn't we have a birthday party, all four of us?"

He was apt to say things like that when he was in high spirits. He'd throw out an idea, no matter how absurd, and laugh himself at the absurdity of it.

"Are you crazy?"

"What's crazy about it? Why shouldn't we make it a family gathering and all have dinner at the Régence?"

"How could we?"

"It's quite easy. As soon as the old cock arrives, we'll burst in, Louise and I, and kiss you on both cheeks, calling you Auntie. . . . That's the idea: we're your nephew and his wife from Nevers, come to look you up. . . . Oh, yes! And we'll bring you a cake, a saint-honoré."

As he spoke, Petit Louis glanced at the old waxwork in the window opposite, whose complete immobility for hours at a stretch was absolutely fantastic. Was that what paralysis was like?

At the same time, he had his ears pricked up for Niuta's door to open, because it was just about time for her to go out for her singing lesson, and he had made up his mind to speak to her in the street.

"What weird ideas you have!" muttered Constance.

"They're quite simple."

No. It wasn't as simple as all that. With Petit Louis, it was a sort of vice: he positively thrived on complicated and equivocal situations. He loved to feel he was pulling strings, with other people, like puppets, at the end of them.

He really did go out to buy the saint-honoré, with Louise trailing along sulkily beside him.

"A jolly party it'll be!" she grumbled. "Without counting the fact that the old man will probably make a special fuss over me."

Petit Louis toyed with the idea of bursting in upon them at the most inopportune moment, but he stopped short of that. When they finally arrived at the apartment, they made quite a touching family scene, with introductions and kissings on both cheeks.

"Monsieur Parpin is a very old friend of mine. He comes and keeps me company now and then, and we talk over old times."

Constance played the game, though her cheeks were flushed, and she couldn't help trembling.

After the first effusions, the conversation began to flag, so Petit Louis suggested a game of belote, which tided them over till it was time to go to the restaurant. They walked to the Régence, Louise and Monsieur Parpin in front, with Constance and Petit Louis following arm in arm.

"I'm so afraid he'll smell a rat."

Monsieur Parpin was no less afraid of meeting his daughter or his son-in-law, and he didn't feel happy until they were tucked away in the farthest corner of the restaurant.

The menu was worthy of the occasion. Caviar (which Louise hated) was followed by lobster *à l'Américaine* and roast chicken, and the feast ended with a bombe. They drank champagne throughout the meal—Petit Louis had seen to that.

"There's only one drink fit for such an occasion," he had stated categorically.

Constance, though she loved to drink, stood it none too well. Before the end of the meal, her eyes were watering and her smile was sentimental. At first, Monsieur Parpin looked worried, presumably wondering what the bill would come to, but he warmed up before long.

"So you come from that charming place Nevers! . . . I was stationed there for a while during my military service. In those days . . ."

The only person who didn't seem to enjoy the party was Louise. Halfway through, she started making signs to Petit Louis. For some time he couldn't or wouldn't understand, but finally he got up from his seat and went off toward the lavatory. In a moment, Louise had overtaken him.

"What's the matter with you?" he asked.

"I don't know. . . . But I don't like the look of things. . . . From where I'm sitting, I can see the whole place in the mirror— right through into the café. There's that inspector again. He's been sitting in a corner all along. He must have followed us."

"What if he has?"

"And then . . . I really can't be sure, but I could swear I saw Gène standing on the sidewalk outside."

Petit Louis didn't flinch. The one thing in the world not to do was to look scared. He wouldn't have admitted he was afraid, even to himself. And yet it had given him a shock. To gain time, he smoothed down his hair, looking in the mirror.

"You're not sure?"

"He was standing by one of the tables outside, talking to some men who were sitting."

"Do you think he's still there?"

"Don't know. . . . But you'd better be careful."

With a familiar gesture, he tapped his hip pocket, then gave a hitch to his trousers.

"Go back now. . . . Later on, get up again. Invent any excuse you like, and slip outside to see if he's still there. . . ."

"Suppose he grabs me?"

Petit Louis shrugged his shoulders.

"Do as I say, and leave the rest to me."

As soon as he was alone, he wiped his forehead. Of course he'd known from the start it was bound to happen sooner or later, but he hadn't wanted to think about it.

There were other things he knew, too. He hadn't played square in taking Louise away from Hyères, for as a matter of fact she really was Gène's girl still. He was in the wrong, too, over the Lavendou affair, because he hadn't been able to resist showing off. Last, and worst of all, he hadn't kept his mouth shut. He'd talked to Constance, who in turn had talked to the chief croupier at the Casino de la Jetée.

If he wanted to be honest, he had to admit that Gène was right in treating him like an amateur—an artist, as he called him.

But they were in Nice now, not Marseille, and a lot of water had gone under the bridge since then.

"I'm going out for a minute.... Do you mind, Auntie?" asked Louise a minute or two after Petit Louis had returned. "I'm feeling a little funny. Perhaps it was the lobster.... Just a breath of fresh air, and I'll soon be all right...."

And from that moment Petit Louis's star began to wane. This was the last time—and the first time, too, for that matter—that he was to sit with his elbows on a white tablecloth in a first-class restaurant, sampling the delicacies of *haute cuisine*, twirling a swizzle stick in his glass of champagne.

He pushed his chair back so that he could get a view of the place in one of the mirrors. And he at once spotted the inspector, sitting over a cup of coffee.

Louise went out. For a moment, he could see her on the terrace outside, and he had the impression that she made him a little sign, which he took to mean:

"It's him all right!"

But he couldn't see her clearly, because between them were scintillating chandeliers and clouds of cigarette smoke.

"I don't think you heard me," said Monsieur Parpin with an indulgent smile. "I was saying that your wife looks like such a sweet girl.... Have you any children?"

Petit Louis's thoughts had indeed wandered, wandered so far from the little comedy they were playing that evening that for a minute he gazed uncomprehendingly into the old man's eyes. And, when he came to his senses, his first impulse was to ask:

"What the hell are you babbling about?"

Instead of which, he answered in a dreamy voice:

"No children ... No ... not yet."

He was no longer alive to the humor of the situation. Everything looked different now. It was as though a cold, crude light had suddenly been switched on them, a light in which Constance and her Pépé looked like obscene photographs, with every blemish thrown into relief, their glaucous eyes greedy for sensation, their falsely ingratiating smiles those of people who feel guilty and try to be disarming.

Constance's head was burning, and her face had turned blotchy. Monsieur Parpin, with his brush haircut and square jaw, must have been a stickler when he was in the customs, and no doubt a martinet to his subordinates, always ready to enforce the rules just where they pinched most.

Louise did not return. If Gène was there, he had no doubt got hold of her and demanded an explanation. In all probability, he had not come alone. He rarely went anywhere without taking the hefty Charlie with him. And hadn't Louise seen him talking to some others?

What would Louise have to say for herself? She could hardly be expected to put up much resistance. She had been in love with Petit Louis, and still was, that was certain. Otherwise she'd never have let him take her away from Hyères, since she knew very well it was asking for trouble.

But there wasn't much fight in her. She wasn't the sort of girl who could stand on her own feet. She was a creature of habit, and she liked security. There was no doubt that, in Nice, she missed the regular, quiet everyday routine of the house, with the afternoon naps in a deck chair on the sidewalk and plenty of popular novels to pass away the time between one customer and the next.

She could hardly fail to be frightened by Petit Louis, who never acted like anybody else, and whom everybody looked at with mistrust.

There was every likelihood she'd go back to Gène. It was true that Petit Louis had bought her—for five thousand francs—but since he'd never paid Gène the money . . .

Monsieur Parpin and Constance looked bored. The conversation flagged. The party, in fact, had fallen flat the moment Petit Louis had ceased to be the soul of it. With restless eyes, he kept watch, and for once he actually derived a little comfort from the presence of the inspector.

If they knew a policeman was sitting there—and Louise would be sure to tell them—they wouldn't dare do anything, because it would give away their connection with him and thus with the Lavendou coup.

A cowardly thought, no doubt. Never mind if it was. Nobody'd ever know. What mattered was to avoid running into Gène and the others outside. They'd take him for a little walk, to some lonely spot along the shore.

"Your wife doesn't seem to be coming back," murmured Monsieur Parpin.

"Pay no attention. It's usual with her."

"I think Monsieur Parpin's getting tired," put in Constance. "And so am I. We're not so young as we were. . . . Perhaps you'll excuse us if we leave you. . . ."

"By all means. Don't bother about me."

Monsieur Parpin paid the bill and murmured a few polite phrases, giving Petit Louis his address in Arles in case he should ever come that way.

Left alone, Petit Louis once more wiped his forehead. Rather than stay where he was, he moved over to the café, not far from the inspector. There he could look out on the terrace. There was no sign of Gène.

The absurd thing was that the lobster really had, in his case, caused indigestion. It was rotten at such a time.

With that thought, he was invaded once more by a sense of personal injustice, and his resentment almost outweighed his anxiety. Why should other people get in his way? He had just settled down to a new life, and he was doing no harm to anybody. He was even beginning to fall in love.

For that morning he had done as he intended and had stopped Niuta in the street. Taking off his hat, he had asked in the sweetest of tones:

"Will you allow me to accompany you for a little way?"

"If you like."

She said it so winningly, and with a broad smile that contrasted with her large, somber eyes. She had a music case in her hand, which he offered to carry for her.

"Aren't you afraid, living all alone in a strange town?"

"Afraid of what?"

"Haven't you any relatives or friends?"

"My mother's singing in New York, at the Metropolitan. . . . She's been here once, when she spent three months in France."

"Why did you lock yourself in the other day, when I wanted to say good morning to you?"

"I don't know. . . ."

It was only a quarter of an hour since he'd arranged the birthday party with Constance. He felt on top of the world as he walked along beside Niuta, who stopped much too soon, saying:

"Here we are! . . . This is where I have my lesson."

She was sixteen. And, sitting in the Régence a few yards from the inspector, he told himself that she was the only real young girl he had ever known, apart from the daughter of the tinsmith in Le Farlet, whom he had seduced in a vineyard, awkwardly, since at that time he knew little more than she did about such matters.

But why should he be thinking of Niuta now? Hadn't he plenty of other things to worry about? If he left the café, and particularly if he got out of range of the inspector's protection, Heaven knew what was waiting for him. Finally, the idea preyed so much on his mind that he went over and sat down opposite him.

"Do you mind?"

"Not at all . . . Is anything wrong?"

For quite a while they were silent. The waiter came up.

"Nothing for me," said Petit Louis. "I've just eaten."

After another silence the inspector murmured:

"Well?"

Petit Louis was dying to find out what the other knew.

"Did you see them?" he asked.

"They were still there ten minutes ago," said the man from the Sûreté, with a jerk of his head toward the terrace.

58

He spoke in the plural. So Gène wasn't alone.

"Do you think they were looking for me?"

"Well, I don't think it was me they wanted," said the other humorously.

"I haven't done anything to them," said Petit Louis angrily.

Louise had not reappeared. That was a bad sign. Petit Louis was getting panicky. He was almost sure the others were waiting for him at a street corner.

"Why are you looking at me like that?" he snarled.

"Because I always thought you'd end up doing something stupid, and I'm more sure of it than ever."

"What do you mean by 'something stupid'?"

"I don't know."

"Then you can keep your mouth shut," retorted Petit Louis, getting up in a rage and going to the checkroom for his hat.

He felt sure the inspector would follow him, in which case he'd be running no risk. Outside, he looked right and left, saw plenty of people but none he recognized, so he set off toward Place Masséna.

It might be wise to spend a few days in the country, his instinct told him.

If he hesitated, it was only to consider the most suitable place to go. Gène and his friends were never away from Marseille long; there they had too many irons in the fire. Petit Louis had three hundred francs on him, because, the evening before, he had taken two hundred from Louise's bag.

He had not yet made a decision when a bus turned the corner, heading for the Promenade des Anglais. It didn't take him a second to make up his mind. He hadn't had time to notice its destination, but that didn't really matter. He jumped on, made his way right to the back, and took out his wallet, feeling more comfortable when he'd counted his money and made sure it was all there.

The conductor stood in front of him. Petit Louis looked up.

"Where does this bus go?"

And, as people stared at him in astonishment:

"I'm asking where the damned thing goes to. . . ."

"To Grasse."

"Then give me a ticket to Grasse. What are you waiting for?"

They must have driven for nearly twenty minutes, and still Petit Louis had made no plans. Suddenly it occurred to him that the others might have seen him jump on the bus and might also have observed its destination.

Without a moment's hesitation, he made his way to the door.

"We're not there yet," protested the conductor.

Petit Louis saw they were approaching a group of lights.

"Shut up!" he sneered as he jumped out.

After walking a hundred yards, he came to a sign that told him he was at Cagnes-sur-Mer. It was half past twelve. On his right was a queer little bar, standing on the main road, and in front of it two big cars were parked. He pushed open the door and, through a thick cloud of tobacco smoke, saw that he was in a small room intersected by a high bar, the rest of the furniture being only three small tables and a few chairs. There was a lot of loud laughter. At the bar were some boisterous Englishmen; behind it, two fat women, who answered as best they could in a mixture of French and English. When they couldn't understand what was said to them, they went into fits of giggles.

Petit Louis sat down at one of the tables and ordered a *menthe* with water.

6

PETIT LOUIS could hardly have been expected to know that from now on every move he made, even the most trifling, was to become more or less historic, that for the best part of a year he was to be called upon to explain actions that he would even have been at a loss to explain at the time he performed them.

When he entered the bar in Cagnes-sur-Mer, he was in a surly mood and not in the least inclined to talk to anybody. And, because he had no liking for Englishmen, there was all the more reason why he should remain quietly tucked away in his corner, especially since one of the women behind the bar had a laugh that jarred his nerves.

The Englishmen were drunk enough to find everything funny. They interspersed their songs with feats of strength or agility, which they performed with neither, and each time they failed, the place echoed with riotous laughter.

It was on a sudden impulse of bravado that Petit Louis stepped forward. Offhand and contemptuous, he asked for a pack of cards, which he tore in two without any apparent effort. He was promptly included in the party and plied with drink, and an hour later he was still showing them tricks, which he explained in a sort of pidgin French accompanied by much gesticulation.

One of them, with sandy hair, was anxious to move on somewhere else. Twice he had whispered in Petit Louis's ear:

"Cinema."

There was a general move toward the door. The women had succeeded in getting their bill paid. The cars outside were started up and a draft of fresh air drifted into the room. Looking out, Petit Louis saw a head protruding from one of the cars, shouting at him:

"Come on!"

He understood that they wanted him to go with them, and, when they spoke again of the cinema, he thought he'd take them to a "special" place on the outskirts of Cannes.

He hadn't for a moment forgotten Gène and the others, but he felt he was giving them the slip rather neatly, and, helped by the whisky he'd drunk, he was once again quite pleased with himself.

When they got to Cannes, they lost a good half-hour by having to wait for the other car, which, for some inexplicable reason, had been delayed. Then they had to find the villa, tucked away on the hill behind. They rang and waited on the sidewalk, looking up at the windows for some sign of life. One of them opened, and a woman, who had removed her make-up, shouted angrily:

"Can't you see we've closed?"

"Isn't Madame Rose there?" asked Petit Louis, who wanted to show the Englishmen he knew his way around.

"I tell you we're closed! And if you go on making a nuisance of yourselves, I'll call the police...."

The cars drove on, and Petit Louis had only a vague idea which way they were going. His companions dozed. They were right in the middle of the Esterel mountains when day began to break.

When they reached Saint-Raphaël, the sky was red in the east. The two cars stopped, and they said something to Petit Louis that he couldn't understand. Then they opened the door for him and pointed to the sidewalk.

They were right in front of the station. By the big pale-faced clock, it was half past four. All was quiet; there was no sign of life, making the streets look too wide.

The cars drove on again, their occupants waving good-by to Petit Louis, perhaps sarcastically. Had they been making fun of him?

He thought it was hardly worthwhile waking up a hotel proprietor, with the night almost over. So they were able afterward to ask him sneeringly:

"Ah! . . . So you were walking around the streets, were you? . . . All by yourself!"

That was just what he was doing. He wandered around alone, past the bandstand and over to watch the little fishing boats going out over the bright smooth water.

He thought things over, as well as a man can think after being up all night and drinking a lot of whisky he's not used to. Once again he told himself that the wisest course would be to disappear for two or three days, long enough for Gène and the others to get tired of hanging around. And, since there was an early bus for Le Farlet, he decided to go to his mother's. He hadn't seen her for four or five months.

For Petit Louis, as for many others, the whole coast from Marseille to Nice, and even on to Monte Carlo, was one vast boulevard that you took for granted, hopping from one place to another on the merest whim.

He had a cup of coffee and a couple of croissants, but in which bar he'd had them was a point he could never remember. The only thing he could have told the jury was that there was a smell of glue coming from the room beyond, and that the man who served him had a shifty look.

Why shouldn't he send Constance a telegram? There was a telegraph office in the station. He wrote rather laboriously, owing to his lack of education.

CALLED AWAY ON URGENT BUSINESS BACK IN THREE DAYS. LOUIS.

Having sent it, he bought the *Eclaireur* and settled down to read it in the bus.

When, later, he was asked whether he noticed anything unusual, he answered no, and thereby enabled the prosecution to score yet another point, for apparently the bus broke down and had to stop for eight minutes at the first turn after Sainte-Maxime.

Buried in his newspaper, he hadn't noticed it. And, absurdly enough, what had engrossed his attention was a story of which he didn't know the beginning and was never to know the end. They had stopped for a full eight minutes and he had never once looked up. It was only at Carqueiranne that he began instinctively to take notice of his surroundings.

They were getting near Le Farlet, which lay on the right, halfway between Carqueiranne and Le Pradet, on a torrid plain where nothing was visible but dark green vines and reddish earth, and an occasional shanty that seemed to have got stuck in the sun-baked landscape like a fly in molasses.

Old Dutto's house, where his mother lived, was outside the hamlet, and Petit Louis took the shortcut along a hedge of canes that was full of the high-pitched singing of cicadas. Some way off, he saw a man he knew, driving a cart. He'd known him as a boy at school, but he was now a hefty man, already inclined to fat. Petit Louis didn't say good morning to him, and the other, half asleep from the rumbling of the wheels, didn't notice Petit Louis.

Another field of vines to cross . . . As always, he came up behind the house, because it was wiser, before going in, to find out what sort of mood Dutto was in. Bending over a tub was a woman of whom he could see little beyond a skirt tucked up to show a pair of stockings tied with red string under the knees.

"Mama . . ." he called.

The woman turned around and blinked, since the sun was in her eyes. Then her only greeting was:

"What have you come for?"

"Nothing . . . Just to say hello . . ."

"That's soon said!"

She had submitted to a kiss on her forehead, but she continued to look at him with mistrust.

"You've been up to some mischief, I bet."

"No, no . . . I was in the neighborhood, so I said to myself . . ."

"So you said to yourself you might be able to get away with a hundred-franc note! No harm in trying, anyway . . . Well, my boy, you've come at the wrong time. . . . I think old Dutto is just about on his way to the next world, and I haven't been able to find out whether he's made a will. . . . Filthy old swine, as I've always known him . . ."

"Where is he?"

"There! . . . Just push open the window."

"What'll he say when he sees me?"

"In the state he's in now, he'd have trouble saying anything."

Petit Louis pushed open the window. Close to it, on a high, old-fashioned country bed, the old man lay with his eyes open, his mouth dribbling, and a cloud of bluebottle flies swarming around his head. There was a nasty smell, like sour milk.

"You don't need to worry. He won't even know you. . . . He's been like that, half living, half dead, ten days now."

She had always had a shrill voice, and if Dutto had been conscious, he'd have heard everything.

"Have you had the doctor in, Mama?"

"The first day . . . He asked if I wanted him taken to the hospital. . . . I didn't want that, because you never know. . . ."

They were surrounded by hens, the same long-legged hens that had been in the yard ever since Petit Louis was little. The old woman wrung out the clothes she had washed and straightened herself painfully, jerkily, rather like a mechanical toy.

"Have you had anything to eat?" she asked, walking toward the house.

"No."

"You know where to find the bread. And there are some salted anchovies in the cupboard."

No place could have spoken more plainly of poverty than

65

that low house, surrounded as it nevertheless was by healthy vines. All the outside shutters were closed. The light, indeed, was so unwelcome that some of them were even nailed shut. Little cats, no larger than big rats, shrank away when anyone approached.

"Have you seen your sister?"

"Not for a while."

"No need to ask what you're doing. It certainly wouldn't be anything to be proud of...."

He said nothing, but he was beginning to get angry. He helped himself to some food and started to eat. He couldn't remember, even as a boy, ever having had a proper family meal in that house, whose occupants went their separate ways. So much did they detest each other that, from the way they behaved, you might have thought you were in a madhouse.

That a row would start before long was inevitable. What actually began it was more difficult to say. She must have said something like:

"I suppose you smelled it!"

"Smelled what?"

"That Dutto was dying. . . . You rushed here as fast as you could, and for once you pretend you're not in need of money...."

"I swear I..."

"I know you as well as if I'd made you myself! If I've got so much as a couple of francs in my pocket, I can count on you to come threatening me, as you did when you were no more than fourteen...."

She had a prodigious memory for things like that. Not a single misdeed had Petit Louis ever committed but she could remember which day of the week it was, what the weather was like, and every other detail.

The incident she referred to could just as well have been passed over as a joke. It was at the time when the first American movies appeared in Toulon, and Petit Louis rode there on the

66

back axles of other people's carriages. He and his friends could only play at being gangsters, but none of them was ever without a piece of black stuff in his pocket to mask the lower part of his face.

Thus masked, Petit Louis had one day pounced on his mother when she was dressing. Half in jest, half in earnest, he had rapped out:

"Give me five francs. . . . Hand over or I shoot. . . ."

He had a toy pistol in his hand, and perhaps he was more carried away by the game than he had originally intended.

She reminded him of it now, ten years later.

"When I think that your poor father, after nine or ten years of work in the mine, didn't even stop at a café on his way home . . . Where you got your bad character from is a mystery to me, unless it was from the Devil himself. . . ."

He started whistling, which only made her angrier. Through the open door they could see old Dutto lying in bed, staring at the ceiling, his features as set as those of the old waxwork who lived opposite the Villa Carnot.

Didn't he ever need anything? Presumably he did, but, since he was quite incapable of saying so, no one could know.

"You're no better than that old carcass there, who's treated me like a slave for twenty years—and done other things besides, things you can't even talk about—and who's now going to die without leaving me a centime. . . . You see if he doesn't! . . . And what's going to become of me then? . . . Instead of having children to help me, I've got a son who spends his life in and out of prison, and a daughter who, now she's got a little money, is ashamed of her mother. . . . In Toulon, once, in the market, she pretended not to see me, because I was squatting there with a basket of beans in front of me, barking out the price to everyone who passed. . . . I don't know whether they'd even take me in a home for old people. . . ."

She wept, but it didn't keep her from talking. The next minute she was off again. Petit Louis had always known her like that.

He knew she had suffered. Perhaps the trek from Lille, with the German armies following, had slightly unhinged her mind.

With age, it had only got worse. Year after year, she and old Dutto boxed up there together—what their relationship was like was beyond imagining. It was well known that he was the most disagreeable man in Le Farlet, and he had always been considered a little queer.

"Listen, Mama!"

"So you wear rings nowadays!"

He had one on his left hand, and of course it hadn't escaped his mother's eagle eye.

"You wear rings like a girl and you . . ."

He must have started swearing at her, and she no doubt answered in kind. It was impossible afterward to remember just what had been said in the incoherent tangle of their arguing, each of them groping for ever more filthy abuse to sling at the other.

Dutto still lay there motionless. And at last Petit Louis completely lost his temper. He had had more than he could stand. His mother had said too much. He grabbed a chair by a leg and began to brandish it around, smashing glass and sending saucepans flying in all directions, the sound of the uproar only feeding his fury.

"I'll be hanged before I ever set foot in this place again!"

"It's not on the gallows you'll finish, my boy. It's . . ."

He strode off, panting, leaving his straw hat behind. He had gone only a few yards when he met, for the second time, his former school fellow, who could hardly have failed to hear the row. Petit Louis ignored him and went on, but the other looked over his shoulder and watched him disappear.

What day of the week was it? Petit Louis really didn't know. His not having been to bed had got the days mixed up. He walked through the hamlet, without taking any notice of anybody, and didn't stop till he reached Le Pradet, where he had a drink in a little bar painted a delicate green. People no doubt recognized him, but he preferred not to speak to them.

68

Jumping into the first bus that passed, he went back to Toulon, where, for lack of anything better to do, he went to a movie.

What else did he do during those two days, of which he was going to be called on to account for every minute. His row with his mother had thoroughly upset him. He had always dreamed of having a mother like those everyone else seemed to have, a mother full of indulgence for her son, pardoning all his failings, and always ready to stand by him in adversity.

He certainly didn't have a mother like that! And he never had had. She saw right through him, and judged him perhaps even more severely than he deserved.

From time to time he toyed with the idea of going straight to the Bar Express in Marseille and having it out with Gène and the others once and for all.

Meanwhile, he bought a new cap in a shop on Quay Cronstadt kept by a former rugby champion who recognized him and thought he was still living in Avignon.

He had only a hundred and fifty francs left, and decided to ask his sister to put him up.

"What's the matter?" she asked when she saw him.

"Nothing . . . Why?"

"I don't know. . . . You don't look at all yourself."

"I'm all right."

His brother-in-law didn't like him, but they nevertheless played belote together until one in the morning. As he had on previous occasions, Petit Louis slept on a mattress in the bar. In the morning he lent a hand, stowing bottles in the cellar. At eleven he had a snack, after which he went into Toulon and played a game of *zanzi* with an Arab, in a bar near the station.

He was bored. He would have liked to know how things were going in Nice. Soon after three, he decided he'd been away long enough, and jumped on another bus. It went only as far as Saint-Raphaël, however. On the boulevard, he thought he saw the car of one of the Englishmen, but he didn't pay any particular attention to it, merely noticing the initials "GB" above the number.

69

He could, the same evening, have taken a bus on to Nice, but there was a fete on, so he stayed and danced, having picked up a little chambermaid from one of the hotels, who reeked of garlic. It was nearly two in the morning when he left her, without having got what he wanted.

This time he slept in a hotel. In the morning, he had a shave at a barber's. At eleven o'clock he got off a bus in Nice and, with his hands in his pockets and a gay sparkle in his eye, made his way to the Villa Carnot.

He had a key to the apartment. Entering the house, he didn't see the concierge, who was rarely in her lodge. On the stairs, he passed nobody. Niuta was once again singing Chopin's "Berceuse."

The door had opened only an inch when he was struck by a queer smell, and the next moment he was standing stock still in the doorway with a worried look, surveying the scene inside. Everything was topsy-turvy, drawers wide open, objects strewn everywhere.

In the bedroom, he almost cried out, for there, lying across the unmade bed, with nothing on but a chemise, was Constance, with her throat cut. There was blood all over her, right down her chest and even on her thighs.

His first impulse was to open the window, because the smell was insufferable. But the idea had no sooner come into his mind than it was succeeded by another—flight. He rushed out and slammed the door behind him, forgetting that the key was still in the lock. The next moment he was in the street, making a superhuman effort not to run, to walk like other people, to breathe naturally.

He walked on and on, to get away not merely from the Villa Carnot, but from the whole neighborhood, which he felt to be dangerous. He was thirsty. His throat was absolutely parched. But it wasn't until he had reached the far end of Avenue de la Victoire that he felt safe enough to stop for a drink.

Going into a bar, he ordered a *pastis* and looked at himself in the mirror behind the row of bottles. His mind hadn't yet begun to work. The *pastis* seemed to him tasteless, and he made such a face when he drank it that the barman asked, in surprise:

"Isn't it all right?"

"Give me something else. . . . Some brandy or some rum . . ."

"Which is it you want, brandy or rum?"

He managed to smile. It was really too silly to lose his self-possession like that, particularly in a bar, and one in which the barman looked anything but a fool.

"I was nearly run over by a streetcar just now," he explained. "It shook me up a little. . . ."

"It happened only last week. An old woman, whose head was cut clean off her body."

Petit Louis was in such a nervous state that for a minute he wondered if the other hadn't invented the story on purpose to upset him. The idea even flashed across his mind that everybody already knew about Constance's murder.

He had quite forgotten, when he left the Villa Carnot, to look around to see if a trap had been laid for him. He went to the door of the bar and looked out, but saw no sign of anybody who might be shadowing him.

"Well, I hope you find the rum all right?"

"Fine, thanks . . . You can give me another."

He swallowed it down and wiped his mouth.

"How much is that?"

He walked on, making a wide circle, keeping well clear of the Villa Carnot. Suddenly he realized, with an unpleasant jolt, that he was right in front of the Palais de Justice, which looked as lifeless as on a postcard.

Finally, in a shady little street nearby, he sat down in a little café, near a large bunch of rosemary; the place next door was a vegetable market. Trying to be calm, he settled down to think things over.

Of course it was Gène who had done it. There was no room for doubt about that. And Petit Louis was more than inclined to think that it was directed against him. It was obvious that, when the body was found, the police would jump to one conclusion: it was the work of the man they knew was living with her.

He had been wrong to run away so quickly. He could see that now. He ought to have looked around carefully, ought to have taken stock of the situation. . . .

Suddenly he jumped, and an icy pang went through him. He felt in his pockets, and realized that he had indeed left the key in the door. Anybody could walk in. The key could easily be proved to be his, because his fingerprints would be on it.

He was tempted to go back for it at once, but by the time he'd paid for his drink he'd thought better of it.

Then began long agonizing hours. Slinking along, sneaking around corners, then pulling himself together and forcing himself for a while to walk naturally, he went from bar to bar, visiting every one in which there was the faintest hope of finding Louise. He didn't dare ask about her.

Three or four times during the day he cautiously approached within a hundred yards of the Villa Carnot, coming finally to the almost certain conclusion that it was not being watched.

Besides, if the murder had been discovered, would they have left the body there? Particularly in the hot weather . . .

He thought and thought, until his head felt as if it was gripped in a steel vise. When he came to a conclusion, he'd start thinking it out all over again from the beginning, only to come to a different one. And each time he reviewed his situation, one fact stood out in ever more ominous relief: he had arrived in Nice with less than a hundred francs in his pocket, and with each bar he called at the sum was dwindling.

He really couldn't tell whether the day was particularly hot, or whether it was just that he himself was hot. Apparently there was some sort of fete here, too, because there were flags in many of the windows, and once he met a band. Perhaps it was Sunday?

Three times at least, he was on the point of going straight to the Sûreté and telling them the whole story. At least he got as far as telling himself he was quite capable of doing it, and that he was quite free to do it—yes, absolutely free!

He repeated the words angrily between his teeth. He saw himself flinging them in Gène's face, and in Charlie's, and he also saw their answering smiles, sarcastic and infinitely contemptuous.

He wouldn't go to the Sûreté, and he knew it perfectly well. He wouldn't go because he couldn't, because something would always hold him back, something that was a mixture of admiration and fear, and also of respect.

That *they* should have done a thing like *that*, just to teach him a lesson . . .

And perhaps all the time they were watching him walking around the Villa Carnot in ever-diminishing circles, sneaking into one bar after another and drinking glasses of rum, which in the end gave his face a tragic, bitter expression.

"Anyway," he groaned, "if I did go, they wouldn't believe me. Nobody would believe me."

And he went on thinking and thinking, fiercely, viciously, haunted by the knowledge that his fingerprints were on that key, and overpowered by the apparent omnipotence of the Marseillais.

In any case, he had to wait until night, and that meant still more glasses of rum and still more wandering along the eternal sidewalks.

7

LATER ON, people whose intelligence was vouched for by degrees and diplomas were to talk gravely about premeditation. What in Heaven's name had premeditation to do with Petit Louis's case? Yet the clever men were armed with chapter and verse to prove it. In particular there were the gloves.

It was nearly eight o'clock when he thought of them, when most of the shops were already shut. He couldn't find any rubber ones, but in a little shop kept by a couple of old maids, who also sold umbrellas, he bought an ordinary pair in chestnut leather.

There was another thing that was to provoke an incident at his trial. It came when his lawyer said, "If Louis Bert"—they were calling him by his full name again, which had hardly ever been used before, since even at school they had called him Petit Louis—"if Louis Bert had not been the only man in his regiment able to carry a side of beef, if he had not been assigned to the butcher shop because of his physical strength, even though he was a cabinetmaker by trade, then he would never have learned how to butcher and he would never have been able to surrender to the impulse to . . ."

And the prosecutor, a little man with a pink face, thinning silky white hair, and a turned-up mustache, jumped up like a jack-in-the-box and shouted, with an indignation that may even have been sincere: "Next you'll be saying that the French army is responsible for the horrible murder of . . ."

And the same people, and others as well, lots of others, were to argue interminably about whether Petit Louis was fully responsible for his actions.

They ought to have been there to see for themselves. If they had, they'd have found a Petit Louis who was quite at a loss to know what he'd been thinking during the last three days, though he should have known if anybody did. Since three o'clock that afternoon, enough had gone through his head to fill a book. And all those glasses of rum he'd drunk, far from intoxicating him, had merely deepened his sense of injury and helplessness. He was a victim, a fluttering insect in a gigantic hand.

There was all that, and much more besides, that those clever people would never understand, like his reaction that morning, or, rather, his failure to react. When he had discovered Constance's body, he had been, more than anything else, annoyed. Then he had fled for fear of being arrested. Then he'd said to himself that it was just his luck to be without Louise at such a moment.

His solitude oppressed him. If he had told them so at the Assizes, the criminal court, they'd have laughed. Yet it was true. His solitude was unbearable, and, come to think of it, he had always been alone. It wasn't the poor woman's fault, no doubt, but his mother had never been to him what other people's mothers were. He could remember perfectly well the day—and he wasn't five years old at the time—when she had said to him bitterly:

"You're the bane of my life!"

The mayor of Le Farlet, a locksmith, couldn't stand the sight of him, and had given instructions to the village policeman to be particularly hard with him.

It had been like that all along the line. And nobody had failed to understand him more completely than the Marseillais, Gène and Company, who had never even suspected that Petit Louis had come to them hankering for comradeship.

And love, for Petit Louis, didn't mean such and such a woman, but the fact of being two together.

"*Basta!*" he used to say when he wanted to banish disagreeable thoughts.

He might well have repeated "*basta*" every minute of that endless day!

The trouble was that, as soon as he'd more or less disposed of one idea, another, even more harassing, would come into his mind. And it only made his torture worse that all around him people were going blandly about their everyday concerns, passing him in the street with their stupid blank faces, without the faintest notion of what was going on in him.

If he left right away, wouldn't he be in time to cross the Italian frontier? There were the fingerprints, of course. But was it absolutely necessary to go back and get that key? Was it Constance's money that Gène and the others had been after? If so, had they found any? Had they taken Louise along with them? Had they . . . ?

A never-ending stream of questions in which the simple facts gradually became submerged and confused. If he could have stopped thinking, it might have been better. But he had to go on, even if his thoughts were merely running in circles, coming back each time to the same starting point.

At all costs, he must remain clearheaded. And once again he started to take stock of the situation. There was a key in a door, his fingerprints on the key. There was a body on the bed. There was blood on the body. There was . . .

He found solutions, then rejected them. He suddenly thought of little details, like the need for gloves, and he remembered there was a strong carving knife in the drawer of the kitchen table.

76

In the wardrobe in the bedroom, there was a large suitcase, which Constance had bought the previous winter, when she went away to watch the winter sports.

There were hundreds of little details like that, thousands of them, which swarmed in his mind, and which he tried desperately to sort out.

For instance, there was the storage receipt for the mink coat. He knew where Constance had put it . . . but did Louise know, too? . . . If she did, there was every chance she'd taken it.

He had no dinner. He couldn't have faced a meal. He waited until exactly half past nine, no later, and then entered the Villa Carnot and walked up the stairs like any other of its inhabitants coming home in the evening.

The police might have been there, lying in wait for him, but when he reached the third floor, the hallway was empty. He put on his gloves, and had just got his hand on the key when Niuta's door opened. The light was behind her, so that he could see her face only vaguely.

"Oh! It's you!"

And, since he found nothing to say, she closed her door again, after muttering:

"I thought you'd gone forever, after that row."

Another thing to worry over! What row had she been referring to? Had Constance put up a fight? And how many people could have heard it, besides Niuta?

On a later day, he was criticized for his inhuman sang-froid. What could Petit Louis say to that? He had done what seemed to be necessary. Certainly he had done it thoroughly. From the time he started, until the job was done, his mind was clear, with a meticulous lucidity that was at the same time deliberate and unconscious.

Thus, when he took the first half of the body in the suitcase, he was careful to wrap it in a blanket, and he waited until half an hour after the movie houses had closed.

His first idea was to throw his load into the sea at the far end of the Promenade des Anglais. But, with no tide to carry it away, and neither wind nor swell, he felt sure it would be discovered within twenty-four hours. On second thought, the port seemed much better. He knew the water must be pretty deep, because quite big ships came alongside the quays.

He had only the one suitcase—besides his own, which he needed for himself—so he had to empty it, and use it for the second load.

Each time, he attached a heavy stone, as you do when you drown a dog. It was nearly four when he got back to the Villa Carnot the second time. Inside, he had to sit down for a while; he was absolutely exhausted.

Mechanically, he lit a cigarette, then poured himself a drink. "Above all," he said to himself, "I mustn't fall asleep."

Then he set to work again, and with such energy that the tenant above banged on the floor to tell him not to make so much noise.

He cleaned and tidied the apartment, going over it methodically, inch by inch, to remove all traces. The bedclothes had gone with the body. And as he worked, he never once stopped thinking about the Marseillais. It was as though he were conscious of their presence.

There was no trace of money or of the most trifling piece of jewelry. On the other hand, he found all of Constance Ropiquet's papers, which he packed in a cardboard box, in his own suitcase with his clothes.

What annoyed him most—for he was still capable of being annoyed—was the disappearance of Louise. Of all that Gène had done to him, that was the cruelest: to leave him all alone, to leave him to an ignominious flight all by himself.

And, after buying the gloves, he was left with fifty francs.

He sat by the window waiting, looking from time to time at the watch Constance had bought him. At exactly six, when the first windows in the neighborhood were being thrown open, he went out and got a taxi. At the door, he said to the driver:

"Keep your engine running."

He had carefully rehearsed his part. Running lightly upstairs, he came down again noisily, carrying his suitcase, threw the front door wide open, and banged on the concierge's door.

"Madame Solti! ... Madame Solti! ..."

He knew she would be asleep and would wake up with her eyes vague, her mind dull. When she opened the little window in her door, she saw Petit Louis standing there with his suitcase in his hand, and she couldn't help hearing the sound of the motor.

"Are you leaving?"

"Yes. We're going away, Madame d'Orval and me. . . . She's out there in the taxi, waiting. . . . We're going to Paris first, then probably on to Holland. . . . I've locked up the apartment. . . . If we're not back by the end of the quarter, we'll send you the rent. . . ."

She seemed to understand it all, and fortunately didn't think of coming out on the doorstep. So she had no reason to doubt that Constance was in the taxi.

"To the station," said Petit Louis to the driver.

As soon as they'd started, he added:

"As quick as you can, please . . . My friend's gone ahead with the luggage. . . ."

At the station, he paid the fare with his last fifty-franc note. The driver couldn't change it and had to go to a café, while Petit Louis waited on the sidewalk.

"Here we are! Eleven francs seventy-five, and the suitcase . . . That makes . . ."

The early-morning sun was shining freshly, and the station was full of life, because two trains had just come in. Petit Louis wandered around for ten minutes, mixing with the crowd, then he dived into the subway and came up in the middle of town.

His first job was to park his suitcase in a café, since he didn't want to have to lug it around. He kept some of Constance's papers with him, including the receipt for the mink coat, which he handed in an hour later at the place where it was being stored for the summer.

He was afraid they might make difficulties, but they merely got him to sign another receipt. He signed the first name that came into his mind: Mariani.

He wasn't feeling tired now. In fact, he was so obsessed by the need to get money that he felt neither fear nor anything else, not even his loneliness. That was the one obstacle still to be overcome. Without money, he could not escape from Nice, where the police took too great an interest in him for him to feel safe.

Shortly after eleven, when, with his cardboard box under his arm, he was on his way to the municipal loan department, he ran right into Niuta as he turned a corner. She was on her way to her singing lesson. Petit Louis was so taken aback that he couldn't think of anything to say. He merely took his cap off very awkwardly and went on, only to realize a moment later that his behavior must have seemed most unnatural.

Shouldn't he have asked her not to tell anyone she had seen him? It was too late now. He ought to have thought of it before. Only, there was too much that had to be thought of beforehand!

At the loan department there were six people ahead of him, and he had to wait. Suddenly he felt tired, overwhelmingly tired, and so giddy he was afraid of falling.

"I've got a fur here . . ."

He had to watch himself closely, because he could detect a rough, brutal note coming into his voice—it was the effect of his fatigue—and he must avoid anything that could annoy people or arouse suspicion.

"Have you got your papers?"

"These are the papers of the person the coat belongs to. . . ."

There! He'd made a mistake! Having looked at the coat and offering ten thousand francs on it, the man took Constance's name and address, and said:

"We'll be sending the lady a check."

He couldn't help asking:

"By mail?"

"Yes, by mail."

Petit Louis was so discouraged that he thought the only thing to do was go and have some sleep. Automatically, he chose the little hotel on Avenue de la Californie where he'd taken Louise when he first brought her to Nice and where they'd spent a night together when Monsieur Parpin came.

They recognized him, saying:

"Has your friend gone?"

"She's away for a few days."

He found the same iron bed, the basin with a large black mark where the enamel had been chipped off, and the glass that had once been a mustard jar.

He went to sleep with a splitting headache. When he woke up, it was the middle of the night, and it took him a full hour to get to sleep again.

Distinguished men, looking at him sternly, were one day to ask:

"And all this time, when you were liquidating your victim's valuables, you never did think of the dead woman?"

No! To be frank, he didn't. There were so many other things to think about. For instance, when he telephoned the concierge of the Villa Carnot, he had to remember all the time to speak faintly, so that he sounded far away.

"Is that you, Madame Solti? . . . I'm telephoning from Lyons. . . . Yes, thank you, Madame d'Orval and I got here quite safely. . . . Listen! Today or tomorrow there'll be a letter for my friend—an important letter, probably registered. . . . Sign for it, will you, and keep it. I'll be calling for it in a day or two. . . ."

He decided to stay in the little hotel, and went to get his suitcase. He had only thirty francs left, which a very indifferent lunch reduced to fifteen. He could, of course, raise some money on his watch, but he knew they wouldn't give him cash, but would send it to him through the mail to comply with regulations.

It was precisely all these regulations that got him down, all these petty frustrations that came between him and the money he needed. For two hours he sat in his room poring over Constance's papers. It was rather like being back in school again, he understood next to nothing about bearer bonds, life annuities, and suchlike.

But he knew that Constance received five thousand francs a month regularly from a lawyer in Orléans. It was to the latter that he now settled down to write a long letter.

Monsieur,

You will no doubt be surprised not to recognize my handwriting, but I've been in a car accident. It was on the Monte Carlo road, and I can't use my right arm at all. So I'm dictating this letter. It's to ask you to send me a money order by telegram for ten thousand francs, in other words, two monthly payments in advance. Please sent it *poste restante* to the Menton post office because I shall be moving almost at once to a nursing home there, only I don't know which one. I have to have an operation.

Thanking you in advance ...

It wasn't until he'd started again three times that he was finally satisfied. As he wrote, his forehead was puckered by a deep horizontal line, and he kept sticking his tongue between his lips. He wished Louise had been there, to go over the spelling, because she'd had more schooling than he had.

Having finished that one, he started on another. He didn't want to, but he told himself he must strike while the iron was hot, and now that he'd got going ...

Besides, he could copy a good deal of it from the first one. There was no more writing paper, so he went out to get some, choosing some of pale blue with a silver border.

You will no doubt be surprised not to recognize my handwriting, but ...

This one was addressed to Monsieur Parpin, asking him, similarly, for ten thousand francs to help with the cost of the operation.

> Don't on any account come to see me now, for my late husband's family are by my bedside, and it would be a disaster if they suspected what we mean to each other. . . .

There was no particular reason why he should ask for ten thousand. It had started with the loan department, where he had been offered that amount on the fur coat, and it seemed to him a nice round sum, so he asked for it again.

If all went well, he'd have thirty thousand with which to go abroad, perhaps to South America, a country which he had often dreamed about.

The only thing that marred the prospect was that he wouldn't be taking Louise with him.

In the evening, his letters mailed, his dinner finished, he had no more than five centimes in his pocket. Wandering around not far from the Jetée, he caught sight of two middle-aged women leaving the casino or the theater. They were strolling along arm in arm, and the idea had no sooner flashed through Petit Louis's mind than he carried it out. He passed them quickly, snatched the handbag of one of them, and ran. A few minutes later, having darted along a number of little side streets, he stopped to inspect his booty.

It wasn't any too good. Three hundred-franc notes, a religious medal bearing the head of St. Christopher, some lipstick and powder, and a handkerchief with a green border. Also a letter in fine handwriting beginning:

"My dear Angèle . . ."

He didn't have the curiosity to read it. Having pocketed the three hundred francs and the medal, he threw the rest into the sea.

That medal, too, was destined to figure in criminal court, giving the prosecutor yet another opportunity to be sarcastic.

"I suppose you counted on the protection of St. Christopher in your efforts to escape the punishment you deserved!"

Nonsense! Hot air! He counted on nothing, neither on saints nor on men. On the other hand, he was too superstitious to throw a saint into the sea.

Still further complications! The next day, when he went around to the Villa Carnot, the concierge duly handed him the letter from the loan department containing the check for ten thousand francs. He tried at two banks, but neither would cash it. Finally, as a last resource, he went into a jeweler's and bought a signet ring with a diamond for five thousand five hundred, offering the check in payment.

The jeweler frowned.

"It's quite all right," Petit Louis assured him. "If you doubt it, you can send it around to the bank to make sure."

He began to feel a supreme contempt for all the multiple precautions with which money was hedged. It wasn't until three o'clock that they gave him the ring, together with the change. Naturally, he had endorsed the check with the name Constance Ropiquet. He had already practiced forging her signature. It wasn't too difficult. Indeed, by the look of it, Constance hadn't done much better at school than he had.

In Menton it was the same. More complications. At the post office, they wouldn't even tell him whether a letter was there, merely saying that, if it was addressed to Constance Ropiquet, she must apply in person.

He hardly knew himself why he'd chosen Menton. Probably because he had once spent the night there, in a brothel. He went to the same place again, and chose the girl who looked most docile. He ordered champagne, and they started talking.

"Would you like to earn five hundred francs?" he asked after a moment.

She was quite willing. So the next day he took her to the post office, having provided her with Constance's identity card. Of course there was a photograph on it, but Constance had chosen an old one, in which she looked no more than thirty, and unless they looked carefully, there was every chance of getting away with it.

The letter was there. The lawyer, like the loan department, had come through. He sent the ten thousand francs asked for, with his earnest wishes for Constance's speedy recovery, and the information that he was hoping to come down to Nice the following month.

They went through the same procedure next day to secure Monsieur Parpin's letter, which began:

> My poor dear friend,
> It was with tears in my eyes that I read your letter, with its truly dreadful news. . . .

A whole page of sympathy and advice.

> when one is no longer young, the bones . . .

Then came the part that interested Petit Louis:

> You know how my children surround me with care, and, to relieve me of all money worries, it is my son-in-law who draws my pension and invests it in his business, in which I have an interest. For my personal needs, he gives me one or two hundred francs at a time—rather like a student's pocket money.
> Fortunately, I have put aside a little, unknown to any of them. It is by drawing on this reserve that I have hitherto been able to send you a little monthly donation, and it is from the same source that I now send you the ten thousand francs enclosed.

Another couple of pages of good advice: what she should eat, what she should drink, not to read too much in bed, not to let the doctors have it all their own way, and just how far to keep the family at bay if she wasn't to lose her independence . . .

And, at the end:

> I hope that very charming nephew and his wife are with you in your trouble. . . .

Petit Louis paid the girl the five hundred francs he had promised her. At the last minute she asked:

"You haven't got me in any dirty business, have you?"

He merely shrugged his shoulders.

For the first time in his life he had nearly twenty-five thousand francs in his pocket.

8

WHAT PETIT LOUIS couldn't possibly have known was that his decisions were already of no great importance, that he was, for the moment, so to speak, under reprieve, that destiny was for the time being forgetting him, giving him scope to go where he wanted, being sure of being able to find him again as soon as necessary.

From his point of view, things seemed to be shaping up pretty well, yet he couldn't shake off a vague uneasiness. It was neither remorse nor fear. In fact, it was impossible to give a name to it. But it nonetheless tarnished his days and took the edge off every little pleasure.

He had money enough to indulge his whims, and he deliberately spoiled himself, as one spoils a child or an invalid.

"You spent enough of your life wearing cast-off clothes," he said to himself.

So he bought himself yet another new suit, as he passed through Cannes. It wasn't the sort of suit a local young man would have bought, but one of those that are only stocked by the luxury shops on the Croisette for sale to tourists. He also bought two or three pairs of shoes, as well as shirts and ties.

The next morning, at the Tour Fondue, he took the boat to the Island of Porquerolles. On board, he went to the front, where he stood, in his new clothes, erect as a figurehead, while two young men in black eyed him enviously.

"All my life," he said to himself, "has been spent along the coast, and all my life I've dreamed of Porquerolles, without ever having been able to get there. . . . Here I am at last, going there, with my pocket full of money, a diamond ring on my finger, and a wardrobe worthy of a rich man. . . ."

He tried to talk himself into being happy. As they approached the island, he looked at the little yellow church among the trees, he looked through the limpid water at the seaweed growing on the bottom. . . .

Still he couldn't enjoy himself. Perhaps the root of the trouble was the fact that he was a gambler. He had raked in twenty-five thousand francs. If he'd taken the first boat to South America, he'd have had enough left to be able to look around for a while when he got there.

But after the first difficulties were surmounted, the ease with which he'd got the money kept him from being satisfied with it. Constance was dead, well and truly dead, and considering all he'd done and how well he'd managed, wouldn't it be unlucky to abandon the game?

He had two good months ahead of him. The concierge had been primed, and wouldn't worry about the absence of her tenant, who, after all, had as much right as anybody else to travel through the world.

He had thought of going to Paris, but the idea didn't attract him at all. He had never been farther north than Lyon, and each time he had gone to Avignon, or Montélimar at the farthest, he'd felt as though he'd crossed a border and was completely out of his element.

So finally he'd chosen Porquerolles. There, he would run no

risk of meeting Gène and his gang, and the local police would take no notice of him.

He disembarked. Mixing with the other tourists, he crossed the square flanked by low houses of many colors. The English all disappeared into a luxury hotel. Petit Louis hesitated, then went on until he found an inn more his own style, with a zinc-covered bar, a slot machine in a corner, and a player piano for dancing in the evening with the local girls.

Outwardly, he was as offhand and sure of himself as on that July day at Le Lavendou when he'd played to the gallery and dazzled Constance Ropiquet.

But it was only outwardly. The buoyancy of that day, the feeling that he was a young god to whom all was permitted, the ease and assurance of movement, thought, and speech, were not to be recaptured.

That had been his one moment of greatness, and every detail of it had been stamped so indelibly on his mind that he could even now have said from just which windows the flags were hanging and exactly how the palms were arranged around the bandstand.

What was so disappointing was the feeling of emptiness, an emptiness that was perhaps really in himself. Whatever he did, he felt he might just as well not be doing it, it seemed so utterly unimportant.

It was in this mood—and perhaps to shake himself out of it—that he decided to bring off a really big coup. He had brought all Constance's business letters with him, and had read them through. One of them from the lawyer in Orléans said:

> M. Robin, who already owns the farm called Loup-Pendu, is very anxious to buy your house in Ingrandes. He called on me this week and offered a hundred and fifty thousand francs for the property. . . . At that price, I think . . .

And in another letter:

You say nothing about M. Robin's offer. I do not wish to press the matter, but . . .

For two whole days Petit Louis turned the project over in his mind, while he strolled around in his pale gray suit and straw hat, watching games of bowls or sipping a drink on the terrace of a café.

Finally, he asked the inn's proprietor:

"You have a typewriter, I suppose?"

"There's one at the Hôtel Miramar."

"Do you think they'd let me borrow it?"

The Miramar was the hotel behind the palm trees he had hesitated to enter. Now, he went there, with a rather involved story, and came away with the typewriter, which had been lent to him for half an hour.

He kept it a good deal longer than that, laboriously picking out the letters with one finger, and constantly forgetting the spaces.

Monsieur,

As a result of my accident I have decided to go to Italy for two or three months for complete rest and change of air. It will cost me quite a lot, and I have decided after all to sell the house to M. Robin. So you can sell it to him for a hundred and fifty thousand francs on condition he pays the whole sum right away. Please see to it at once and send the check to me at Porquerolles, where I am staying at the moment.

I am dictating this letter because I am not yet recovered, though I can now use my hand a little.

Hoping to hear from you shortly . . .

And he signed: Constance Ropiquet.

It was really quite simple. But he didn't know how Constance wrote to her lawyer, nor was he sure what terms one ought to use when speaking of the sale of a house.

He read it through again and again, hesitated, then went out to mail it, hesitating again before dropping it in the box. He had given his address at the inn, and had said to the proprietress:

"I'm expecting my cousin shortly. Constance Ropiquet is the name. If any letters come for her, will you let me have them?"

He had nothing to do now but wait for the answer. He enjoyed himself meanwhile with the money he had, which was enough to enable him to take on anybody at poker dice or belote, and stand rounds of drinks without counting the expense. He had clothes enough to excite the envy of the local boys when he swaggered around the square.

He knew they envied him, knew they tried to walk like he did and copy his easy movements at bowls. The tourists, too, turned around to look at him, particularly the older women, like Constance.

When they danced in the evenings, it was generally admitted that he could waltz better than anybody.

What more could he want? He set out, almost systematically, to gratify every old and unfulfilled desire, some of them dating from his childhood, some of them absurd, such as the wish to smoke nothing but gold-tipped cigarettes.

Sometimes, during the heat of the day, he lolled on the imitation leather banquette near the zinc-covered bar, and if he was alone with the servant girl who also was the waitress, he would carry on a desultory conversation with a sentimental expression on his face.

When she admired his ties, he gave her three, and he promised her a lizardskin belt like the one he was wearing, which he'd bought in Cannes.

"No boy friend?"

And, with a satisfied smile, she let him flirt.

But beneath all that, something was gnawing at his insides, something Petit Louis did not want to admit, even to himself. It was a sense of humiliation.

It made him try to be clever. He swaggered around, playing to whatever gallery of fishermen and other small fry he could gather around him, but all the time he had the feeling that he had demeaned himself.

It wasn't that he ought to have gone and denounced Gène to

the police. As a matter of honest fact, that had been out of the question from the start. And for more reasons than one. First of all, it wasn't the thing to do, and also it would have got him nowhere. Moreover, Gène and his kind were in well with all sorts of people in Marseille, including politicians and others who could pull strings, and they'd have had little difficulty in getting back at him.

No! It wasn't that. . . . What he ought to have done, what he would have done if he'd been a man, was to go and hunt up Gène in Marseille. He should have sauntered casually into the Bar Express, and, looking him straight in the eye, said in an ominously quiet voice:

"I've come to settle accounts."

One hand, of course, in his right jacket pocket, with the muzzle of his revolver showing through the cloth.

Gène would have answered with a joke, to gain time. The others, sitting at the little round tables, would have sensed at once that this was serious.

One for Louise! . . . One for the old girl! . . . Another for . . . Six rounds! One, two, three, four, five, six—all fired from his pocket. Then a dash into the street and a breathless chase down little streets and back alleys.

He hadn't done it! Instead, he was showing off to all the youngsters of Porquerolles, and making passes at a servant girl who was cunning enough to smile sweetly and lead him on, without having the faintest intention of letting him go too far.

On receipt of your letter, I at once wrote to M. Robin telling him you were prepared to consider his offer and asking him to call on me at his earliest convenience. I am now awaiting his reply.

They had given him the letter addressed to Constance Ropiquet without any difficulty. The sight of her name on the envelope plunged Petit Louis into gloom. Sitting in the shady café, looking out at the little yellow church across the way, he had received a gust from Nice that brought memories of lazy life in the little apartment with flowered paper on the thin walls, through which floated Niuta's voice, of a wide-open window, and, opposite, an old waxwork who sucked a pipe that never smoked. . . .

He ground his teeth and swore eternal hatred of Gène, hatred all the more painful because he knew he would never assuage it, would never dare even to try. Because they were stronger, and he was afraid of them.

Around ten o'clock each morning the boat arrived. Petit Louis, in his pajamas, dawdling over breakfast on the terrace, would get up and stroll across the square to buy a paper, waiting his turn in the crowded little shop.

He always took the *Eclaireur*, because it had all the news from Nice, but he had never found any that concerned him. This was not surprising, since there wasn't one chance in a thousand of a ship's anchor fishing up the remains.

Even if that happened, how could they ever identify them? . . . But what was the use of going over all that again? . . . Constance was dead and gone, and nothing he'd done that night was of any further importance. . . . All the same . . . There were certain details . . . For instance, when he'd looked around for something to use as a hammer and his eyes had lighted on the electric iron.

What else could he have done? . . . Once started on the job, what choice had he but to see it through? . . . What sense would there have been in letting himself get nabbed for a crime he hadn't committed, with the almost absolute certainty of being convicted?

No! The only thing was not to think about it. You can worry an aching tooth, if you like, but you can't play around with memories like these. Or, if you do, there must be something wrong with you. There were some things . . . Well, you just wonder how you could ever have done them. . . .

"*Basta!*"

He usually succeeded in banishing the gruesome visions from his mind. It was much easier than forgetting Gène and Louise.

93

Of the latter he'd had no news and presumed she was once more back in that house.

He read all the local gossip of Nice, while swallowing his coffee, which was now cold. Then he went to dress, whistling as he climbed the stairs. From then on, the day was his, a clear hot day, like all the others, in a universe scaled down to this miniature island.

He didn't count the days. It didn't occur to him that summer vacations cannot go on forever. Impatiently, he waited for the hundred and fifty thousand francs. With those in his pocket, he could choose the life he wanted. Meanwhile, he didn't even make plans.

One evening, he tried to enter the servant girl's room. Calmly, without any show of indignation, she refused to open the door, and he went away angry. After all, he'd spent the best part of five hundred francs on her! The next day he had sat for a long while in the sun, and the morning after he woke up with a violent headache.

He had no forebodings, no thought that, on the mainland, the papers had been out since four o'clock, and that a consignment of them was gradually approaching in the leisurely little steamer.

"Did you have a good night?" asked the servant girl with a grin.

Petit Louis shrugged his shoulders and turned away sulkily, chose a table, and sat down to wait for his breakfast. Soon, a little crowd of people approaching told him the boat had arrived. He gave the news dealer time to sort out his papers, then strolled over for his copy of the *Eclaireur*. For a quarter of an hour he was buried in the first two pages, which gave the general news. Then, on the local page, he saw:

MYSTERIOUS DISAPPEARANCE FROM THE VILLA CARNOT
POLICE SUSPECT MURDER

Why should the electric iron instantly leap into his mind? There were a hundred and one other details he could equally well have thought of. Yet, before he'd even started to read the article, he was convinced the iron would play the major role.

94

He had taken every imaginable precaution. Ten times, at least, before leaving the house at six o'clock, he had looked all around the apartment to be sure no clue was left behind.

Often since then he had made a mental tour of the rooms, asking himself the same question.

And all of a sudden he knew he had forgotten the iron. He had forgotten it—it was almost as if he could see it—on the lower shelf of the little bedside table, where he had put it, meaning to go back to it later. It was just at the very worst moment, when he was on the verge of being sick and had to go to the window for a breath of fresh air.

He sat there, holding the paper, but not reading it. The article stared him in the face, but all he could see was an electric iron. At the next table, a young woman in shorts was dipping her buttered bread into a bowl of chocolate.

Oddly enough, it was Niuta who was the cause of it all. She had gone out as usual about eleven o'clock. Half an hour later, the Swiss doctor who lived three doors along the hall called down to the concierge:

"There's some gas escaping somewhere. You'd better see about it."

The concierge came upstairs. She knocked on two or three doors. A little group gathered in the hall, and someone suggested:

"It's probably from Madame d'Orval's. Is she still away?"

"She won't be back for another month or two," declared the concierge.

There was a lot of confusion. Everyone seemed determined to make the most of it, to prolong the pleasure.

"You haven't got a spare key, Madame Solti?"

"No! The young man has one, but he took it with him."

"Oh, yes! The secretary!" a fat woman observed scornfully.

"Perhaps we'd better get a locksmith. . . ."

But the Swiss doctor bent over the lock.

"The keyhole's much the same shape as mine. Wait a minute; I'll try my key."

He had guessed correctly. It fitted perfectly. Till then, nobody had suspected that at least a dozen doors in the house had locks that were identical!

The little group entered.

"What a funny smell!"

"It's stuffy, certainly. But there's no smell of gas."

They weren't going to miss this opportunity to explore someone else's apartment.

"It seems bigger than ours. Don't you think so? . . . I thought all the apartments were the same."

"Not quite, because of the balconies."

"Do they both sleep in the same room?"

"Of course not. There's the little room beyond."

They were turning to go, to continue the hunt elsewhere, when the concierge tripped over an electric wire and nearly fell. One end was attached to an iron, which she picked up to put somewhere else.

"Looks like hair . . ." she muttered.

She looked with disgust at the dark crust on the iron to which some hairs were stuck.

"What did you say?"

"I said it looks like . . ."

And the Swiss doctor, who was as nosy as any of them, leaned forward to inspect the iron.

"They certainly are hairs," he affirmed, "and I'd swear they were Madame d'Orval's. She came once to consult me. And that dark stuff . . ."

"You're not saying it's . . ."

"I'm saying it's blood, and that this iron's been used for . . ."

Five minutes later, the concierge returned with the policeman from the corner. He cleared the apartment and shut the door, then sent for the inspector.

The latter asked a few questions and called the Sûreté.

The excitement lasted all day, with many comings and goings: the police medical expert, the head of the Sûreté, and finally, at about five o'clock, a whole host of experts, examining magistrates, and court clerks.

The escape of gas had been entirely forgotten, and it was Niuta who, when she came back at half past twelve, found her little stove half on.

The police seemed to be everywhere. A dozen times the concierge was called up to the apartment and plied with questions, which were usually the same.

"But I told you already! They went off in a taxi first thing in the morning. I heard the motor with my own ears."

"Did you see them?"

"I tell you, the young gentleman woke me up to tell me they were leaving. . . ."

"So you saw them?"

"As plainly as I see you now!"

"And you saw Madame d'Orval, too? . . . I mean Madame Ropiquet. . . ."

"Why don't you call her Madame d'Orval? Everybody does."

"Did you see her?"

"Yes."

She wasn't lying, but she said it with a slight hesitation, as though she felt at fault. The truth was, she wasn't quite sure.

"It's a question of the utmost importance. Think it over carefully. Are you quite sure you saw Madame d'Orval that morning?"

"Yes!"

Too bad! It was better than contradicting herself.

"How was she dressed?"

"I didn't notice."

"Did she speak to you?"

"I don't remember. . . . No. I don't think she did."

"Didn't she say good-by?"

"How can I remember? You'll drive me crazy with all your questions. And while you're keeping me here, my little girl's all alone downstairs."

The *Eclaireur* didn't give all these details. Only a general out-line, with an old photograph of Constance Ropiquet, which the police had found in one of her drawers.

It ended with:

> The police are anxious to know the whereabouts of the victim's secretary, Louis Bert, known by the name Petit Louis, who has already been convicted twice.

Sitting on the café terrace, Petit Louis read the words without moving a muscle. When he got up, it was to go back to the news-paper seller.

"Have you got the *Petit Var* and the *Provençal*?"

He looked through them, standing, but there was nothing in them. No doubt their Nice correspondents had telephoned the news too late.

"Have you got any copies of the *Eclaireur* left?"

"Only one. For the chef of the Grand Hotel . . ."

"Do you sell many?"

"Eight."

Petit Louis remained perfectly calm. He was amazed at him-self. As he stood in the shade of the eucalyptus trees, nobody could possibly have suspected. . . .

The boat had just left, on its return trip to the Tour Fondue. It was too late to take that one. There was another at two. Or he might get away earlier by hiring a boat. There were plenty in the port.

"You were very unkind last night," he said sadly to the little servant girl.

It really did make him sad that she should have been unkind to him.

"See that my bill is made ready, will you?"

"You're going?"

He almost said:

"Unless they stop me!"

Afraid of letting his tongue run away with him, he turned on his heel and went up to pack his bag.

98

9

HIS ROOM LOOKED OUT on the square, and the windows were open. Surrounded as it was by shady eucalyptus trees, the center of the square, glaring in the bright sunshine, looked like a little lake. Glancing across it, as he threw his clothes hastily into a suitcase, he saw the door of the post office open.

It was directly across, near the church. A nervous man hurried down the steps and crossed the square diagonally, making for the humble little building that served as town hall.

Petit Louis had no need to see which newspaper it was that the postmaster carried in his hand. Even in the distance, when he was little more than a silhouette, his movements were so eloquent that Petit Louis stopped packing. He could have sworn the man was talking to himself. He could almost see him inside, seizing the policeman by his buttons and bursting out with:

"Do you know who's here? . . . The man who murdered that woman in Nice!"

Quite unruffled, Petit Louis went on staring out the window. Then he looked impassively at the crumpled suits he had crammed into his suitcase.

He was caught. The police would certainly get him long before the afternoon boat. And if he got away in a hired boat, where would he go? All the ports along the coast would be warned to be on the lookout.

He looked in the mirror, pleased with himself, with his calmness, and with the bitter smile he brought slowly to his lips. Then he shrugged his shoulders and turned toward the stairs, muttering, with a sigh:

"Poor old Petit Louis!"

It was the only time he softened. Downstairs, he strolled into the café, and, with a steady hand, lit a cigarette. That reminded him that the servant girl had also admired his lighter.

"Here!" he said. "Keep this! . . . Maybe someday the sight of it will make you regret last night. . . ."

"What? . . . Still harping on that?"

Of course she couldn't understand how much it meant to him. The room was almost empty. Two sailors, with the name of an English yacht embroidered on their shirts, were dozing in a corner. Soon the policeman appeared in the square, hurrying like the postmaster.

"Give me a tomato, will you?"

This meant a pernod with a drop of grenadine. He didn't often drink alcohol so early in the day, but he wanted once again to sniff the smell of pernod.

"What are you staring at?" asked the girl.

"That's the mayor, isn't it, talking to the policeman?"

"Yes. . . . Why?"

The mayor was also the grocer. He had a heavy dark mustache and wore a gray smock like an ironmonger or a linotype operator. The two men stood in the sun, deep in discussion.

Petit Louis had nothing to do but wait. He wondered whether the two men outside would be bold enough to tackle the job, and he smiled when the policeman at last took leave of the mayor and advanced to the entrance of the café, his right hand on his revolver holster.

"Come in, Bonnet!" called out Petit Louis, who had more than once stood him a drink.

The policeman was embarrassed.

"Do you answer to the name Louis Bert?"

"I would not deny it."

"Louis Bert, I have a painful duty to perform and I must ask you not to make it harder. But I'm bound to tell you that I will be obliged to shoot if you make the least move. Now, hold your hands up."

Petit Louis couldn't help smiling again, and, as he held up his hands, he winked at the girl.

"Handcuffs already?" he asked in gentle reproach.

In the square outside, a dozen people were gathered around the mayor. Bonnet led his prisoner over to the little building, which boasted only two small rooms, and which nobody would have suspected of being the town hall, had it not been topped by a flagpole.

Bonnet was being very decent. It was, of course, a very serious moment for him. Next morning, the arrest would be in all the papers.

"Go in!" he said politely to Petit Louis, opening the door of his office. Rolled up in a corner were the flags used for state occasions. There were also some Chinese lanterns and some fireworks left over from the celebration of Bastille Day.

"Sit down. . . ."

He shut the door behind him, and then, when curious faces appeared at the windows, he closed the shutters, too, so that they were left in near darkness.

"Of course, I haven't got a warrant for your arrest, but I'm sure it's my duty to keep you in custody until I phone Hyères for instructions."

"Certainly," said Petit Louis encouragingly.

"It's a more delicate matter than you seem to think. You see, I didn't catch you *in flagrante delicto*."

He seemed happy to have somebody who could appreciate

these subtle problems. In fact, he really couldn't help treating Petit Louis as a distinguished visitor. As he telephoned, he kept looking at him in a way that was more respectful than reproving.

"Is that Hyères? . . . The Police Superintendent . . . Hello! . . . Can I speak to the super? . . . Hello! . . . Is that you, sir? . . ." (Here a wink at Petit Louis.) "I have the honor to tell you some important news. . . . It's about that Nice affair. You know about it, don't you? . . . Well, I have the murderer in my office now. . . . Would you mind telling me what I should do? . . . Yes . . . Right! . . . Do nothing until I hear . . ."

He hung up and turned rather shyly to Petit Louis.

"I don't think I have a right to question you officially," he said hesitantly. "The superintendent will call me back when he's had instructions from Nice."

It was cool in the little room, which was dominated by a picture of the president of the Republic and a dusty Marianne smudged with ink. Suddenly Bonnet threw open the shutters and roared:

"If there are any more demonstrations, I'll clear the square."

And so it went, up to three o'clock, in an atmosphere of cordiality. Then two armed policemen arrived to take the prisoner back to the mainland. One of them was young, smart, and freshly shaved, and, as far as he was concerned, Petit Louis had nothing to complain of. The other, however, was fat, flabby, and unhealthy-looking, with one shoulder higher than the other. He immediately went up to Petit Louis with a surly look.

"So that's him, is it? The little pimp who goes around murdering old women!"

At the same time, he deliberately trod with all his weight on Petit Louis's toes. The latter looked at him steadily, without wincing.

"What's this? Won't you say how do you do to me?"

Bang! His right hand caught Petit Louis squarely on the cheek. But Petit Louis still said nothing, merely spitting on the ground.

"Well? What have you got to say?"

There was no need to say anything. The man needed no provocation, though that was obviously what he was after. Finally, giving up the attempt to goad Petit Louis into insulting him, he took off his coat to beat him up.

Petit Louis never flinched. When the operation was over, his upper lip was swollen and he had a nasty wound on his left temple. His tie had been wrenched away and the collar of his shirt was torn.

"We'll take care of that pretty face of yours! See if we don't."

At five, the two policemen took him down to the boat. It was only a couple of hundred yards to walk. The crowd of onlookers was clustered in little groups, silent and affected. So they left with proper dignity.

The policemen must have been afraid Petit Louis might jump overboard, because they took him down to the saloon, which smelled of fuel oil. The passengers had to remain on deck.

Reinforcements were waiting at the Tour Fondue: a police lieutenant and a sergeant with a car. Half an hour later, they reached Toulon, where they went to the station and boarded the Paris-Nice express.

Petit Louis had had nothing to eat or drink since eleven that morning, but he would have bitten his tongue out rather than complain.

At Nice some fifteen reporters and photographers were waiting at the station, and he was hustled into a car, which delivered him to the Sûreté a minute or two later.

For nearly an hour he was kept waiting, sitting on a bench in a room where several plainclothes men eyed him with curiosity, then went on with their work. They talked and telephoned, they came and went. Around ten o'clock some beer was brought in, but nobody thought of offering any to the prisoner.

At last a bell rang. One of the men got up and beckoned to Petit Louis.

"Come!"

A padded door was opened. Standing waiting for them was a man with a round body and no less round a face. His nose was round, his eyes round, and beneath a soft mouth was a small round chin with two additional ones beneath it.

"You can leave us, Janvier. . . . Shut the door, will you? And I don't want anybody to disturb me."

Petit Louis saw, sitting in a corner, another man, whom he immediately recognized as the one who had called at the apartment and whom he'd spoken to at the Régence. He stayed in the background, as though he was merely there as an observer.

As Petit Louis already knew, his real name was Mine, but he had been nicknamed Minable by his colleagues because of his seedy appearance. He was dull, colorless, and badly dressed, never very clean or well shaven. His yellow teeth gave him bad breath, and anyone he talked to was bombarded by a fine spray of saliva.

"Sit down, Petit Louis. . . . Here! Have a cigarette. . . ."

Monsieur Balestra, the head of the Sûreté, paced up and down the room, wondering where to begin. He struck a match for Petit Louis, who was still handcuffed, then went to the desk and picked up a sheet of paper.

"By the way, this is the warrant for your arrest. . . . I know lawyers love to trip one up over matters of procedure. . . . To make sure, we telegraphed the warrant to Porquerolles at three o'clock. So, you see, everything's quite in order."

Sitting in his corner, Minable was pretending to study his notebook, a particularly grubby one with a rubber band to keep it shut.

Petit Louis was thirsty, but for nothing in the world would he have shown it. He looked hard and stubbornly at the two men, as though he was not in the least afraid of them.

For the first ten minutes there didn't seem to be anything particularly dangerous in Monsieur Balestra's questions. Not that Petit Louis was for a minute taken in by his affability, since it wasn't the first time he'd been questioned by the police, and he knew some of their tricks. After each question, he paused for a moment to reflect, and he couldn't help from time to time looking inquiringly at the seedy Minable, as though some bond existed between them.

They could hear the reporters in the next room talking in loud voices while waiting impatiently for the result of Petit Louis's interrogation. One of them was telephoning to his paper in Paris and was shouting so loud that every syllable could be heard.

"At the present time, the wretch is being subjected to the able interrogation of Monsieur Balestra, the head of the Sûreté in Nice. . . . Balestra . . . B for Bertha, A for Arthur . . ."

Petit Louis smiled, and Balestra was forced to do the same. His smile turned to a look of annoyance, however, and he got up and went to the door.

"A little less noise out there!"

Necks were craned to get a glimpse of Petit Louis sitting in front of the chief's desk. Then the door was closed.

"I was asking how much she paid you a month."

Petit Louis frowned. This was now the third or fourth question that hadn't seemed to him quite natural. No doubt there was a catch in it somewhere, but just where it was, he couldn't make out.

"I didn't have a fixed salary."

"On piecework, I suppose," said the chief, grinning. "Now tell me which day it was that she gave you that diamond ring."

"How should I know? Probably one day when she had won a bundle at the casino."

"She played for pretty big stakes, didn't she?"

He didn't know what to answer. He knew very well she didn't. What could it matter anyway? Yet Balestra seemed to think the question important, since he repeated it.

"Played for big stakes, didn't she?"

"She may have. I wasn't with her all the time."

"Of course not. You had her accounts to keep. You were her

secretary first and foremost, and anything else was just thrown in. . . ."

No. Petit Louis didn't like it at all. By half past ten, he hadn't been asked a single one of the questions he'd expected. Not even the principal one! Apparently it hadn't once occurred to them to ask him:

"Did you kill Madame Ropiquet?"

Or:

"How did you do in the old girl?"

Nor had there been the faintest allusion to the raid in Le Lavendou or his relationship with Gène and Company. Not a word about the birthday party, which Minable had witnessed.

It was almost as though the latter hadn't told his chief about it. But that was obviously absurd, since he was here in the room. What was he here for anyway? And what were all these questions leading up to?

"I'd like to make a statement," growled Petit Louis, with a dark look at the inspector in the corner. "Anyway, that gentleman can tell you that . . ."

"All in good time!" interposed Balestra. "You'll be given every opportunity to make a statement. In fact, you can make as many as you like. But for the moment it's I who am putting the questions, and all you've got to do is answer them. Now, in the wallet the policemen took from you this afternoon, I found this receipt from the local loan department. It's dated August 23rd and made out to Madame Ropiquet. That means that she was alive on that date, since she pawned her fur coat. . . ."

No answer. Petit Louis would have liked to have a pencil and paper, so as to get the dates clear in his mind. Day after day he had been aimlessly whiling away the time at Porquerolles and he'd never thought of sitting down to work out the exact sequence of events.

"Do you follow me? On the 23rd she pawns her coat and she gives the receipt to you to keep. No doubt she's afraid of losing it herself. And after all, it's only natural if you're her secretary. . . ."

Petit Louis's attitude had undergone a change. With his head right down on his shoulders, his neck had almost disappeared. He seemed compressed, as though to gather all his strength, and mistrust had brought a foxy look into his eyes.

"What do you say? Did she give you the receipt?"

"What if she did?"

"Do you admit it?"

"Suppose I do. . . ."

When were they going to come to the point? When were they going to ask him about the murder, about the body?

Not yet!

"So on that day, the 23rd, you were both in Nice. In the afternoon, to be exact. On the other hand, according to the concierge, you left at six in the morning in a taxi for the station. . . ."

Petit Louis's eye did not waver. Balestra got up from time to time and wandered around the room, playing with a little box from which he now and then took a lozenge, which he deposited gently on his fat tongue.

"Of course it's really for the examining magistrate to clear up all these little details. I'm only going over the ground roughly for my own personal information. . . . Did you then take a later train, in the afternoon or evening?"

Petit Louis's upper lip was beaded with sweat. He knew very well that, whatever he said, that night was irrevocable, that it was with the answers he gave now that they'd try later to corner him.

"What train did you take?"

"I can't remember."

"There are people who thought they saw Madame Ropiquet wearing a blue dress in the ten o'clock train."

This was not true, obviously, for at that time Constance was already in two pieces at the bottom of the harbor. But that didn't mean it was a silly statement. On the contrary, everything Balestra said had a reason. The thing was to guess it.

"You called Madame Solti from Lyon. From which hotel did you telephone?"

"From a public phone."

"In the post office?"

"No. In the station."

"Which station?"

"The big one."

He hadn't been in Lyon for a long time and had forgotten the name of the main station, Lyon-Perrache.

"Was it a public telephone?"

"Yes."

And, in the corner, Minable continued studying his notebook as though it contained the Ten Commandments.

"You're not too tired? Shall we finish it off tonight?"

"Whatever you want!" sneered Petit Louis, who had never been so thirsty in his life.

"I suppose the policemen gave you a bite."

"This sort of bite!" sneered Petit Louis, pointing to the cut on his temple.

"You're not hungry? . . . Or thirsty?"

"Whatever you say!"

He knew what he was doing. He wasn't going to wheedle for a sandwich or a glass of beer. Balestra went out of the room, and for a moment they could hear the buzz of conversation among the reporters. Petit Louis thought Minable would say something to him, but he remained as mute as ever. Hadn't the chief gone out precisely in the hope that Petit Louis would open up to the inspector?

Balestra returned.

"They're bringing up some beer. . . . Now! . . . Where were we? . . . Oh, yes! What was the idea of going and burying yourself in Porquerolles? . . . They say it's a very pretty place, but all the same . . . Though of course you'd be quite near your mother there. She lives at Le Farlet doesn't she?"

It was wearying the way he jumped from one thing to another. What on earth did his mother have to do with it? What were they getting at? And how much did they already know?

"Isn't that old Dutto dead yet?"

"I don't know."

"When was the last time you saw her?"

"Some time ago."

"A month?"

"I don't know."

"I've telephoned to Le Farlet and told them to let your mother know that, if she wants to see you, she can come any time she likes, and I'll give her permission to visit you in prison."

"She wouldn't be able to come."

"Why not?"

"She has to look after Dutto."

A waiter from a neighboring café came in with the beer, and at last Petit Louis was able to drink. So thirsty was he that he could have drunk all three glasses. But the effect of the cold liquid was that he burst out into perspiration all over.

"What was it you were supposed to be buying her?"

"Who?"

"Constance Ropiquet."

"I don't understand."

It was half past eleven, and there wasn't a breath of air in the room. It was so stuffy that Balestra took off his coat.

"She can't have pawned her fur coat for nothing. Obviously she was in need of money. She must have needed about twenty-five thousand francs for something. That must have been about what you had on you when you landed in Porquerolles."

"So what?"

"Perhaps she wanted to buy a little cottage on the island?"

"There's no reason why she shouldn't."

He didn't want to commit himself. He was struggling to steer his way through all the traps and pitfalls that were set for him, and the effort hardened his features to the point of making another man of him.

Gone was the good-looking athletic boy who strolled around casually, with his hands in his pockets, a white cap at a rakish angle, and a disdainful smile playing on his lips.

In his place was a stocky, thickset man from the North, the

son of one of those tenacious miners who can work for hours and hours at the coal face without ever sagging for a moment.

"We'll come back to that another time. . . . At least, the examining magistrate will. . . . Really, I think the case is quite simple, and the inquiry will soon be closed."

Was Balestra making fun of him? What inquiry was he talking about, since he'd never once referred to Constance's death? On the contrary, every time he had mentioned her it had been in a way that would lead one to suppose she was still alive.

And the seedy Minable, who had been on Petit Louis's track in the first place, because of the Lavendou affair . . . Yet there had never been the slightest hint of that. . . .

"You can take it easy now. . . . Tonight you'll sleep in the lockup, and then tomorrow we'll find a cell for you in the prison. . . . Have another cigarette?"

For the next half hour Balestra was busy with his papers. He put through two or three telephone calls, which had nothing to do with Petit Louis's case. Then he called his house to say he wouldn't be back until two or three in the morning.

"Well!" he said at last, with a sigh. "Let's get back to our business. We both want to get it over with, don't we? . . . As usual, work always comes in a rush. . . . Now, about that money . . ."

And at half past two they were still at it, and there had been no mention of any murder, or body, or electric iron.

It had been nothing but a stream of trivial questions about the time of departure of a train, how a particular sum of money had been spent, or a date over which Balestra and Petit Louis couldn't agree.

"Well, good night! Till tomorrow . . . Or, rather, I don't know when, since it's the examining magistrate who'll continue with the case . . . There's one thing: your lawyer won't be able to say I've handled you roughly. . . . A cigarette?"

He called in two men, who marched Petit Louis off, and that was all for that day.

10

IT MIGHT PERHAPS truly be said that with that night in the Sûreté, and only then, Petit Louis's real life began, his own life, according to his own allotted destiny.

He had been a very ordinary baby, messy and always covered with scabs—not that that mattered very much, since nobody ever thought of kissing him.

At the school in Le Farlet he had gained no distinction, and later, as a cabinetmaker's apprentice, he had been neither promising nor unpromising. And so it went. . . .

And now everything had suddenly become significant. All the trivial details that nobody had paid any particular attention to at the time were dragged out of their oblivion and pieced together like a jigsaw puzzle to make a picture.

For a whole month, Petit Louis knew nothing about it. Only once had he been taken before the examining magistrate, and then the scene had been short.

The magistrate was a dry, methodical sort of man named Monnerville, who was so absorbed in his papers that he found no time to look at Petit Louis.

"I have called you here to notify you of the charges laid against you: murder, theft, forgery, using a forged document, and embezzlement."

He read them out, apparently anxious not to forget one.

"The law prescribes that you may from now on be assisted by a lawyer of your own choosing."

When Petit Louis did not answer, he at last raised his eyes, without surprise, without the least spark of interest in the person standing before him. In fact, he looked at Petit Louis, whom he was seeing for the first time, exactly as if he'd seen him every day for years.

"I beg you to inform me which lawyer you would like," he went on in the same voice.

"Who's going to pay him?"

"It will be at your expense, naturally."

"Will they give me back the money they took when they arrested me?"

Even for so simple a question, Monsieur Monnerville found it necessary to consult his papers.

"It will be returned to you if it's proved to be yours."

Petit Louis shrugged his shoulders cynically.

"Well?"

"I won't have a lawyer."

"Then I'll have one officially assigned to you."

With these last words, he made a little sign to the guard at Petit Louis's side, and the latter was led away without having had a further view of Monsieur Monnerville's eyes.

After that, every time his cell door opened, Petit Louis asked: "Has he sent for me again?"

Finally the guard said:

"You seem in a terrible hurry! The longer it drags on, the better you should be pleased."

"Why?"

"Oh! Never mind!"

But at the same time he winked at the prisoner who shared Petit Louis's cell. The latter was an Arab who never stopped talking, laughing, and joking the whole day long in a way that wasn't quite natural.

"What did he mean?" asked Petit Louis.

It was simple enough! Only Petit Louis did not know that every day at least two columns appeared about him in the papers. Twenty reporters were snooping around, independently of the police, producing daily another crop of sensational revelations or another hitherto unsuspected witness, whose photograph would be splashed on the front pages.

And all the while Petit Louis was wondering why he wasn't being interrogated, why he hadn't even been asked whether or not he confessed to killing Constance.

As for being in prison, he accepted that philosophically, even good-humoredly, and, though he never spoke to his cellmate unless it was to snap at him, he was always ready to crack a joke with any of the guards.

Sometimes, in the morning, he would lie full length in the triangular patch of sunlight that was thrown on the floor, and, shutting his eyes, he would dream of the Villa Carnot, of Niuta's singing, of the old waxwork opposite and his canary.

Porquerolles, too, was a happy memory, clear and cheerful, like the memory of some fete.

At other times, he spent hours getting all his facts straightened out and making up his mind what he was going to say.

He had been arrested on September 13, and the same night he had been questioned by Balestra at the Sûreté in the presence of the seedy Minable. It was three days later, on the 16th, that he had been taken before the examining magistrate, Monnerville.

And it wasn't until a month later, on October 15, a day when it was raining cats and dogs, that he was taken in the prison van to the Palais de Justice. What he couldn't understand was why he was taken in through a little door at the side, and why he was hurried by four policemen up some back stairs and along deserted corridors and pushed as quickly as possible into the magistrate's room.

He was ignorant of the fact that, in the main corridor, a crowd of reporters and photographers was being held in check with difficulty, and in the street outside, where he was expected to arrive, more than a hundred people had been standing in the rain for the last two hours.

On the way, he had been winding himself up, so to speak, in order to be all ready for the fight, and he walked into Monsieur Monnerville's room like a wrestler stepping into the ring. The room was badly lighted, and in the gray gloom his eyes fell upon a tall young man in robes. He guessed at once that this was his lawyer and he accordingly studied him with a critical eye.

He wasn't an ace, certainly. They weren't going to give him, gratuitously, one of the leading lights of the bar. One might even think that this young man was somewhat intimidated by his client.

"Your lawyer, Maître Bouteille, will be present whenever you are being questioned and will have access to the papers concerning the inquiry."

Petit Louis sat down, and his brow contracted into a frown at the sight of the examining magistrate, who with an intensely studious air was turning over the pages of the dossier, a dossier that seemed to contain hundreds of pages.

Ten minutes later, he was wondering whether he was really there; whether it was really he who had led the life being painted with disconcerting precision.

"At the age of nine," recited the magistrate in his even, toneless voice, "you were expelled from the village school, and it was only thanks to the intervention of the mayor of Le Farlet that you were readmitted. . . ."

Petit Louis had expected anything but that. He sat motionless, his eyes riveted on the face of this Monnerville, who seemed hypnotized by the pile of papers on his desk.

"I will now read you a statement made on oath by your former teacher Ernest Ceccaldi, to Inspector Merlin, the same being duly commissioned to conduct an inquiry. . . ."

It was agonizing. Petit Louis wiped his forehead, because he had broken out into a sudden sweat.

". . . On the other hand," the voice went on, "Monsieur Edmond Grimaud states: 'I never trusted that young Louis Bert, and when he was thirteen I caught him playing bowls with a pair of balls that had been stolen from me the previous week. If I said nothing about it at the time, it was only out of consideration for his poor mother. . . .' "

Then, in a slightly different tone:

"Do you admit having stolen a pair of balls?"

Between his teeth Petit Louis muttered:

"To be so unlucky!"

"What's that?"

"Nothing, Monsieur. Go on. I'm very interested. . . ."

A sarcastic smile came to his lips, which curled a little more each time he heard a particularly imposing passage.

Patiently, Monsieur Monnerville unfurled his dossier, which, though he never stopped reading, he seemed to know by heart. Passing straight from one item to the next, he never had the curiosity to look up to observe Petit Louis's reactions.

The lawyer, who had his back to the window, was taking notes in a tiny notebook, using a gold mechanical pencil.

"Your first employer was Jean Morzenti. . . . Will you tell me why you left him?"

No answer.

"I repeat: will you tell me why you left him?"

"Why bother to ask? I'm sure it's all written down there. . . ."

"Morzenti states: 'Petit Louis was in my employment six months, and as far as his work was concerned I have no complaint to make. But he had a bad influence on my son, whom he used to take with him to all the fetes in the neighborhood. And then when I found that money was constantly missing from the house . . .' "

So it went on—hour after hour. A whole procession of people called up from the past, always snarling, always accusing. One might have thought that Petit Louis was the only person in the world they'd ever known, so clearly could they remember his most trifling acts and gestures.

There were some who, after the lapse of eight years, could give the exact date and hour of such and such an event.

"At sixteen you had a liaison with a married woman, whom you turned away from her conjugal duties. . . ."

At that, Petit Louis fairly exploded. Nobody could have told whether he was laughing or crying. His eyes glistened.

"Monsieur Magistrate!" he pleaded in the tone of one deploring an exaggeration.

"Do you deny it?"

"But, Monsieur Magistrate, that woman came to Le Farlet for the summer and stayed a hundred yards from our house. She was thirty-five. . . ."

"I don't see what that has to do with it."

"Well, as you said yourself, I was sixteen—as a matter of fact, I wasn't even quite that—and if the law has anything to say about it, it should prosecute her for seducing a boy under age. . . ."

"You're not called upon to make any comments."

"Perhaps I might say . . ." began the lawyer.

"Maître," broke in the magistrate in a tone that brooked no contradiction, "I beg you to allow me to conduct this examination as I think fit. If you consider it improperly conducted, you'll have ample opportunity for saying so at the Assizes, and I have no doubt you will do so with your usual success."

A slap in the face for Maître Bouteille, who had, two days before, defended a client who was given the maximum sentence.

After this, the even voice flowed on once more:

"Madame Patrelle, a friend of your mother's . . ."

"You don't say!"

The old Patrelle woman! The meanest old hag in Le Farlet. A woman who spent her time writing anonymous letters.

"Silence! . . . Madame Patrelle states: 'That poor Madame Bert has had many misfortunes to bear, seeing that she was driven from her home by the Germans, and many a time she has said to me that of all her troubles the worst was having a son like

Petit Louis, who often frightened the life out of her. And once she added that she was sure he'd end up cutting her throat. . . ."

The room was too small for all the host of spirits that were conjured up. The whole village was there, male and female, young and old, jostling each other, surging forward in an ugly crowd clamoring for Petit Louis's blood. There was even a schoolfellow who wasn't quite all there, who declared that Petit Louis had once taken him to a brothel, and that the women there seemed to know him well, since they all called him by his Christian name.

There was no end to it. Like everybody else, he had lived the days of his life once, thinking that they were then over and done with. Not at all! They now had to be lived through all over again, with this difference: that it was no longer he who chose what he would do or how he would do it. It was other people!

And what distressed him more than anything was the mournful formula:

> In pursuance of the written instructions of M. Monnerville, Chevalier of the Legion of Honor, examining magistrate appointed to the Public Prosecutor's Department in Nice, we Augustin Grégoire, police inspector in Avignon, did on the 28th day of September . . .

All over the place, inspectors and simple policemen had been patiently and laboriously collecting every fragment of Petit Louis's life and writing it all down, richly interlarded with official phraseology, of which the examining magistrate never skipped so much as a syllable. He read it all out word by word right down to the:

> Witness my hand this . . . day of . . .

To think that for a whole month this work had been going on without Petit Louis hearing the faintest echo of it! Lying in prison, he had pictured them searching indefatigably for Constance's body, and what he feared more than anything was to be asked point blank:

"Why did you throw the remains of Constance Ropiquet into the harbor?"

The weight of all these depositions was absolutely crushing. His head was empty, his throat parched. And there were no glasses of beer here, as there had been at the Sûreté. The rain poured down steadily. People passing along the corridor were hardly audible, and no doubt Monsieur Monnerville had given orders he was not to be disturbed, even for the telephone.

"To continue . . . Up to the age of twenty-two you appear to have frequented brothels in the capacity of a customer. . . . You certainly had a considerable leaning for such places. Your successive employers have testified that you spent most of your free time in them. . . ."

"That could be said of a great many people!" grunted Petit Louis.

"What did you say?"

"Nothing . . . Go on."

Monsieur Monnerville was on the point of flaring up, but he thought better of it and went on:

"At twenty-two you turned up in Avignon, and it was there, in one of these places, that you made the acquaintance of a certain Léa. . . ."

It was unbelievable! In Petit Louis's eyes justice seemed like a monstrous machine, a sort of colossal grinding machine.

They'd even fished up Léa! Léa, with whom he made his modest debut in the pimp's trade. He was still working at the time, and she used to give him a little pocket money because he amused her. She was a good-natured girl, easily entertained. He used to tell her stories by the hour, and she never failed to laugh at them.

"The woman Léa, now in Algiers, has made the following declaration. . . ."

And Petit Louis nearly came out with:

"*Merde!*"

He was now holding himself in only with difficulty. It wasn't just anger that was invading him, but a terrible uneasiness. They had him on ground on which he could find no foothold. Nothing seemed to have any firmness or consistency left in it, not even the magistrate sitting facing him, or the walls of the room, or this lawyer of his, Maître Bouteille!

"It was one day when you were visiting this Léa that you met another woman, Louise Mazzone, with whom you were soon on intimate terms. The two women had a fight and Louise Mazzone retreated to Marseille, where she entered another house of the same sort. . . ."

He couldn't make head or tail of it. In a sense, it was true, and yet it wasn't. They'd chosen to put it in a way that made it completely false. It wasn't because of the slap that Léa had given her, in front of clients, that Louise had "retreated" to Marseille.

"I must ask you to stop me if there's any fact you don't agree with. . . ."

"Go on, Monsieur Magistrate."

The interrogation had begun a few minutes past two. It was nearly five by the time they got to Hyères. The magistrate seemed ready to talk of everything except Constance Ropiquet and her manner of death.

Then suddenly:

"In July the police find you in Nice, installed in the apartment of a Madame Ropiquet, a lady of private means, who frequented the Casino de la Jetée, where she passed herself off as Countess d'Orval."

Petit Louis jumped. He opened his mouth to speak, but said nothing after all.

What made him jump was something very fishy, no doubt a trap, anyhow something dangerous. After all that detailed story of his life, Monnerville had suddenly skipped several weeks of it.

They had been out to find everything they could against him and had spared no pains to unearth every petty offense of his childhood. And yet not a word about the episode in Le Lavendou. He'd been questioned by the police on that occasion. Why wasn't that in the dossier?

No! They didn't seem to want to know where he'd met Constance. They just took it as a *fait accompli*.

"... the police find you in Nice ..."

It was because of the raid in Le Lavendou that the seedy Minable had been on his track, knowing that it was only through Petit Louis that he could lay his hands on the other culprits.

"You then bring your mistress from the brothel in Hyères where she was working, and you oblige Madame Ropiquet to accept that abominable situation."

Petit Louis smiled, suddenly wondering why he had got so upset about it all. The whole thing was too stupid. The case was cooked from start to finish. For instance, in saying nothing about Monsieur Parpin. . . . And then the way they described Constance as a woman of private means.

Admittedly she was, up to a point, but that didn't alter the fact that she received regular monthly payments from the retired customs official. So, when all was said and done, she plied the same trade as Louise Mazzone!

The concierge knew all about it, and would have been sure to tell the police.

"It was on Friday, August 19, that Madame Ropiquet was last seen, namely, at the Régence, accompanied by you and Louise Mazzone."

"Excuse me ..."

The magistrate lifted his head.

"Who said that?" asked Petit Louis.

"I have before me the report of a police inspector."

"In other words, Mine."

"It's of no importance. He happened to be in the Régence and he saw you ..."

"Didn't he see anybody else?"

Monnerville pretended to scrutinize the report.

"There's no mention of anybody else."

"I would like to know why the fourth member of the party is left out. For there were four of us. We were celebrating Constance's birthday."

"I must ask you to refer to the victim as Madame Ropiquet."

"Whatever you say. But that doesn't change the fact that there was another person with us, a certain Monsieur Parpin. But I suppose his being a high-up civil servant . . ."

"Be quiet! . . ."

Petit Louis was standing, thoroughly worked up again. His lawyer got up, too. It looked as though they would all come to blows in a minute.

"Just look at that!" sighed Petit Louis, sitting down again. "I know plenty about Monsieur Parpin. A vicious old man if ever there was one! . . ."

"Once more, be quiet, or I will call the guards!"

"Don't think you can frighten me."

Petit Louis was still touchy. Monsieur Monnerville, flustered, rattled on:

"I note that there was a fourth person present, and I shall consider the advisability of calling on him to give evidence."

"And that's about as far as you'll go!"

"To return to what we were discussing . . . She was last seen . . ."

Petit Louis now made a great effort to listen, but his temples were throbbing, and his shirt was sticking to his back.

"For the remainder of that night, no trace of you can be found. The next day, Saturday, in the morning, you arrived at your mother's house, or, rather, that of Monsieur Dutto, in which she is employed as a servant. I will now read the deposition of Madame Bert. . . ."

Petit Louis trembled. He looked at his lawyer, as though to ask him whether this was legal.

Question: Were you expecting a visit from your son?
Answer: No.
Q: Did he often come unexpectedly?
A: From time to time, and it was always when he needed money.
Q: Did you notice your son approaching the house?

A: No.

Q: Were you indoors or out?

A: In the yard.

Q: It is possible, then, that he deliberately approached the house in such a way as not to be seen?

A: It would be just like him.

Q: Suppose he had been carrying a heavy suitcase and had wanted to hide it?

A: I didn't see any suitcase.

Q: But you didn't see him come. Did you tell one of your neighbors that you didn't find him quite natural?

A: I may have.

Q: What did you mean by that? Did you say anything about his having been up to something bad? Think carefully. Remember that the neighbor in question has made a statement under oath.

A: I really can't remember just what I did say. . . . Perhaps I did say he must have been up to some mischief again.

Q: Pardon me! The statement I referred to said "up to something bad." Was it "up to some mischief" or "up to something bad"?

A: I don't see much difference.

Q: Very well . . . Now, did your son ask you for money?

A: No.

Q: So you don't know why he came to Le Farlet?

A: I don't know.

Q: He might have come to hide something without your knowledge?

A: It's possible, but I don't think so.

Q: Why?

A: Because I don't think he killed that woman. If you let me see him for five minutes, I'll soon know whether he did it or not. I can come to Nice now that old Dutto is dead. And if he did do it, I'll be the first to say so.

At that moment, Monsieur Monnerville looked up and said very quietly to the guard sitting by the door:

"Bring the witness in."

Petit Louis was afraid to understand. He looked at the magistrate, then at the policeman, at his lawyer, and finally at the door. With clenched fists and staring eyes, he watched the dark figure veiled in mourning who came into the room.

11

ONE COULD NOT FAIL to be aware that beneath her voluminous draperies and unknown number of petticoats was nothing but the thin scraggy body of an old woman. Her veil was so thick that it was impossible to say what she was looking at, and Monsieur Monnerville, trying to make his voice sound sympathetic, said:

"I'm afraid I must ask you, Madame Bert, if you'd be so kind as to uncover your face."

A gloved hand drew back the crepe, revealing a lined face with a yellowish complexion and pale eyes that glanced furtively at Petit Louis, anxious not to encounter his. One might have thought that Madame Bert was afraid of her son, as certain people, who are not used to them, are afraid of the dying. She looked at him with sidelong glances, as though he already belonged to another world, mysterious and awe-inspiring. Then, realizing he hadn't changed, that he was still the same Petit Louis as ever, she fumbled for her handkerchief and began to cry.

"I'm extremely sorry to impose this ordeal upon you, but in the interests of justice . . ."

Petit Louis entrenched himself behind a grim, hostile immobility. There was hardly a quiver of his nostrils as he gazed with a fixed stare at the examining magistrate.

"If he did that, it'll be the death of me," groaned the old woman, sniffling. "I can't believe it. I can't believe that God would give me this to suffer on top of all I've been through. . . . If you only knew, Monsieur Magistrate . . ."

She whimpered in a way that gave her old face a childish expression. It was difficult to believe she had once understood life and even been full of life herself. She was now no more than a phantom draped in black, cringing before the new disaster that had befallen her.

"Calm yourself, Madame. I'm going to ask you one or two questions, even though you may already have answered them when you were interrogated by the police. . . . Look at me, please."

Obediently, she raised her head, and, since politeness demanded it, she even produced a wan smile.

"Take your mind back to the last visit your son paid you. What was it you said next day to your neighbor?"

Madame Bert cast an anxious glance at Petit Louis, then a second one, which seemed to say:

"Too bad for you! It's only the truth! . . ."

And she answered:

"I think I said he didn't seem quite natural."

"Didn't you say something about his having been up to something bad?"

"Whatever I said, I never thought of anything like *that*. . . . I thought he might have been in some brawl or other. He was always getting into fights. When he was little, he was always coming home with cuts and bruises."

The tears began to flow again.

"If you knew what I've had to put up with all my life, Monsieur Magistrate . . ."

Petit Louis was determined not to look at her and he gazed

intently at Monsieur Monnerville's mahogany desk, the top of which was inlaid with green cloth.

"What you have suffered has been largely on account of your son, hasn't it?"

She nodded.

"Since August 20 you haven't found anything around the house or in the fields that your son could have brought there?"

"Nothing at all, Monsieur Magistrate."

Timidly she turned to look at Petit Louis, but it only set her off on another fit of weeping. In response, he made a slight movement of his arms, a movement that was immediately arrested by the handcuffs. His nostrils twitched. His eyes were fixed on the magistrate with such intensity that the latter cleared his throat to cover his embarrassment.

"You have several times said that your son threatened you, which implies you thought him capable of assaulting you. What exactly was it that you feared?"

The whole drama was written on Petit Louis's face. Dogs subjected to vivisection, dogs who have believed in the kindness of man and who suddenly feel the sharp jab of the scalpel, dogs who suffer and to whom nothing is any longer understandable, must have just such a look in their eyes as Petit Louis had then and just such a rush of blind homicidal anger to their heads.

"What exactly was it that you feared? . . ."

And the old woman didn't know what to answer. She wanted to be polite to the magistrate, but she felt awkward in front of her son.

"One says things like that when one's angry."

"Has he never threatened you?"

"Only with a toy pistol. It was only in fun. . . . He was too young to understand."

"Nonetheless, he was always pestering you for money, though he knew you had none to spare."

Madame Bert hung her head and sniffled. Then she began again, as though she was reciting a litany:

"I've always been unlucky, always! . . . Even during my husband's life, poor man, who ought to have been in a sanatorium instead of down in the mine . . . And now—would you believe it, Monsieur Magistrate—people point at me in the street and children throw stones. . . . Dutto's dead, and do you know what happened? . . . A nephew of his came from Italy, plunked himself down in the house, and told me to clear out. He hardly gave me time to pack my things. . . . And what's to become of me now? The newspapermen are at me all day long, trying to make me say things I don't mean. . . . I've only got my widow's war pension, since nobody seems to want to give me work. . . ."

It was the lament of a child, of one whose mind has been completely submerged in her sorrows. She glanced quickly at the magistrate and Petit Louis as she spoke, as though looking for signs of pity.

"I don't know what's to become of me. This is all I have left. . . ."

She rummaged feverishly in her bag while the embarrassed magistrate made a sign to the guard.

"I must thank you, Madame, and once more say how sorry I am to have troubled you. . . . We won't want you any more for the time being."

He got up and bowed to her as if he were in a salon.

"Before you go, I must ask you to sign the minutes of this confrontation. . . ."

She bent over the paper the clerk handed her. When she had signed, Petit Louis jumped from his seat and called:

"Mama!"

They remained face to face for a few seconds, weeping, both of them, then Petit Louis turned his head away and muttered hoarsely:

"I swear I didn't do it. I swear I didn't kill her."

When he looked around again she was no longer there. Outside, in the corridor, she was being assailed by reporters and photographers.

"Now read out the minutes," said the magistrate imperturbably to the clerk, "and get the prisoner to sign them. . . . Unless, of course, he prefers to be sensible and make a confession. . . ."

He had finished his day's work, and a hard day's work it had been. Getting up from his desk, he went over to a closet, inside which he started washing his hands.

Petit Louis had changed. The stubborn, crafty look that had come into his eyes during his interview with Balestra had been fixed there forever by Monnerville's interrogation.

The next day, the Arab they had foisted upon him was in his usual joking mood, and Petit Louis coldly and deliberately decided to have him removed, and there was only one way to do it.

He was lying on the cell floor, as on other mornings. The Arab, who lacked three front teeth, was laughing his particularly nauseating laugh, and Petit Louis calmly got up, seized him by the neck, and with his free fist started bashing his face.

His lip was cut at once, and the sight of blood, far from appeasing Petit Louis, only spurred him on. As a matter of fact, as he lashed out, he wasn't really thinking of the Arab at all, but of the examining magistrate, and of all sorts of other things he could never have put into words.

Roused by cries, the guards rushed in, and, after rescuing the Arab, four of them set upon Petit Louis.

That didn't matter. He wasn't afraid of blows. The important thing was that the Arab was taken away and he was left alone.

That's what he wanted. To be left alone, gloomy and surly, to stew in his hatred of the ways and means of justice. Ever in his mind's eye was that monstrous dossier, every leaf of which bore the testimony of some man or woman who had been sought out and picked up like a piece of rubbish from a garbage heap for no other reason but that they had something to add to the stink.

There were more to come, surely. Petit Louis's lips curled at the thought. They'd said hardly anything about Louise Mazzone, still less about the concierge, and Niuta hadn't been mentioned at all.

But then, the magistrate hadn't come to the murder yet. No doubt he was leading up to that. Slowly and cautiously! A very thorough man was Monsieur Monnerville!

As though to prove it, a week went by without any resumption of the inquiry.

Petit Louis's hope of being left alone was not gratified for long. Another man was dumped into his cell, this time a Yugoslav who couldn't speak a word of French. He was huge, a veritable monster, with formidable muscles and arms hairy as an ape's. A religious emblem hung around his neck over some indecent tattooing.

Petit Louis understood. They had chosen somebody who wasn't so easy to knock around. The two men made no attempt at friendship. They lived their separate lives as though the cell was divided by a stone wall.

The attitude of the guards changed, becoming rougher. What Petit Louis didn't know was that this was merely a reflection of public opinion, whipped up to indignation by the newspapers.

Moreover, the police were annoyed with him because of their failure to discover Constance Ropiquet's body, or any other serious evidence except in support of the charges of forgery and theft.

"It begins to look very much like the perfect crime," one reporter wrote.

So Petit Louis appeared to the public in the guise of a man of exceptional intelligence and rarely equaled coolness.

Monsieur Parpin was dead. Nobody so far had mentioned his name. In just one paper there had been a vague reference to an old friend of Madame Ropiquet's, but nothing more. Nevertheless, the poor man had ended by swallowing—accidentally, it was said—a strong dose of Veronal.

Petit Louis knew nothing of that. He hadn't seen his lawyer

again. Each day was his to put his ideas in order. Strangely enough, he was getting fat, which didn't suit him at all.

Fifteen days had passed before the prison van once more took him to the Palais de Justice, and it happened to be another rainy afternoon.

He sat down in the same place as before and looked coldly at the magistrate, who had two files in front of him this time, the yellow one that had been there before and a red one, which was new.

His lawyer was there, like a clerk in an office, attentive but unconcerned, and Petit Louis noticed that there were two policemen on guard instead of one, at which he smiled contemptuously.

"Today I want you to explain your relationship with Louise Mazzone, who has been found in a private house in Béziers and who has been questioned."

Petit Louis remained alert, saying nothing.

"I'm waiting for your answer."

"What did she tell you?" snarled Petit Louis.

And when the magistrate didn't answer, he went on:

"I suppose you've got her there behind the door, to spring her on me the way you did with my mother!"

"I must ask you to adopt another tone; otherwise I shall have no course but to send you back to your cell."

"All right."

"I have asked you to enlighten me concerning your relationship with the woman Mazzone."

"Isn't it plain enough? Do you want me to draw you a picture?"

"Perhaps it's not so plain as you wish to make out. . . . Guard, bring in the woman Mazzone."

Of course! He'd guessed it! They wanted to play the same trick on him as they had the other day. Louise came in, wearing a little winter coat and looking as modest as any working girl. By the polite way she bowed to the magistrate and the lawyer, it looked as if she'd studied her part beforehand.

"Take a seat, please. . . . I have before me the report of your interrogation by the police inspector of Béziers, and I would like your confirmation of certain points in the presence of the prisoner."

She nodded assent, while Petit Louis pretended to be thinking of something else.

"You have declared that at first Petit Louis was just one of your customers, though a regular customer, and that it was only later that he became attached to you. . . ."

"That's right."

"So, at that time the prisoner did not belong to what the papers refer to as 'the underworld.' "

"He never did belong."

"Why not? Is it a fact that the gentlemen of the underworld didn't want to have anything to do with him, regarding him as an amateur?"

"They didn't feel they could trust him."

"For your part, were you attached to him?"

"The thing is, he wanted to 'get me out of it,' as he used to say. He used to make out I was unhappy there, and he'd give me a new life."

"Was he working at that time?"

"Not regularly."

"Not regularly. I take note of that! What happened then?"

"I left the Marseille place to be with him, but I soon found out we had nothing to live on, so I went back to business in the house in Hyères."

"Did you hand over your earnings to him?"

"No. But when he came, I used to give him a little, because he was always broke. I had my other man then. . . ."

"We don't need to go into that," put in the magistrate hastily. "It has no bearing on the case."

Petit Louis looked up and smiled, a smile that expressed all the contempt in his heart.

Not once did Louise turn toward him, and he was never able to get a good view of her.

"Go on."

"He kept trying to get me to give up my life and go with him. Then one day he came and told me he was being looked after by a rich aunt in Nice and that I could come, too."

"He said an aunt?"

"I would never have gone otherwise. It was when I found out the real way it was that I left, because I felt sure it would lead to no good."

"You foresaw what would happen?"

"Well . . . not exactly . . ."

"What do you mean?"

"That Petit Louis isn't like anybody else. You never know what may come into his head. I knew he'd get me mixed up in something that wasn't right, like making me have dinner that time with the old man. . . ."

"I must request you not to bring in the gentleman, who's now dead."

Louise quickly apologized.

Petit Louis looked up in surprise, because this was the first he'd heard of Monsieur Parpin's death.

"Did Petit Louis and his so-called aunt often quarrel?"

"Now and then."

"I suppose it was about money?"

"She certainly wasn't always as generous as he'd have liked."

"In short, you preferred to go back to that house rather than get mixed up in a situation that seemed to you shady."

"That's about it."

"Thank you. That's all I have to ask you. If you'll just sign the minutes . . . I take it, Louis Bert, that you've no objections to raise to the very clear and precise evidence we've been listening to?"

At the mere sight of Louise's face, opposite, Petit Louis felt forced to say, in a low voice:

"I'd like to know how she can believe the woman was my aunt, when the three of us used to make love together."

She trembled and then, turning to the judge, stammered out:

"I don't know what he's talking about."

And the judge retorted, severely:

"I do not wish this proceeding to take an unnecessarily salacious turn."

The whole thing was a put-up job. He had suspected it for a long time; now he was sure. He was so disgusted that he didn't even turn to watch Louise walk sedately to the door.

"Is that all?" he muttered disdainfully. "Do you want me to sign, too?"

The magistrate's face went crimson and he shouted:

"There's only one person here who has the right to ask questions, and that is I."

"In that case, you might perhaps ask me whether I killed Constance! And the answer is that I didn't, and you're just fooling yourself!"

"Silence!!"

"It's about my turn to say something. . . . I'm the one that it's all about; I'm the one that's in prison, and you won't even tell me what you've got against me. . . ."

Monsieur Monnerville banged the desk with his fist. Then the lawyer intervened:

"As a matter of fact, Monsieur Magistrate, it might be just as well if you asked my client . . ."

"Excuse me, Maître. You can intervene as much as you like at the trial, but this is my inquiry and I'll conduct it in my own way. And what's more, I'm not going to stand any improper behavior from this impossible individual."

Petit Louis laughed, then looked at the magistrate as much as to say:

"You can have your inquiry! And you know where to put it!"

To punish him, they let him cool his heels for half an hour while the magistrate went and had a glass of water and was buttonholed by the reporters.

At a little bar around the corner, Louise Mazzone found Gène and Charlie waiting for her with a car, in which all three drove off.

When the session was reopened, Monsieur Monnerville pronounced with dignity:

"I trust I shall be allowed to finish this inquiry in the way I consider seemly. We have two more witnesses with which to confront the accused: first of all, Laure Moneschi, prostitute, registered in Menton, who, on August 24, at the instigation of Louis Bert, presented herself at the post office and produced the identity card of the deceased. . . ."

The lawyer, who had two or three times tried to break in, at last managed to say timidly:

"Excuse me, Monsieur Magistrate, but we have no proof of Constance Ropiquet's death. . . ."

Petit Louis couldn't help looking ironically at the young lawyer, who had at long last said something to the point.

They brought in the woman Moneschi, who, in contrast to Louise, was flashily dressed in shiny purple. She was fat and gentle, spoke with a lisp, and was obviously a confirmed chatterbox.

"When he didn't undress, I asked him why he'd come upstairs, and it was then that he said he'd rather talk. And he asked me if I'd like to earn five hundred francs. 'Only if it's aboveboard,' I said, and he swore on his mother's head . . ."

"I beg your pardon!" interrupted the magistrate severely.

"Well! He swore it was. And I had no reason not to believe him. . . . I've got a little girl boarded out with some people in Piedmont, and of course that costs money. It was thinking of her that I agreed."

"Louis Bert, do you contest the evidence?"

"I made use of this girl to get hold of two letters and to cash a money order for ten thousand francs, but I didn't kill Constance Ropiquet."

"That's all I have to ask you. Will you sign, please," the magistrate said to the girl.

"Then it's not true?"

"What are you referring to?"

"They told me I was being had up for . . ."

"I'm satisfied you acted in good faith. Sign here. . . . Yes, your real name . . . Thank you."

"Can I go back to Menton? Because, you see . . ."

"You can return to Menton. Guard, show this person out and bring in Mademoiselle . . ."

He had to look for the name in the dossier.

"Mademoiselle Niuta Ropichek. And tell the other witnesses that I won't be able to hear them today. They will be notified when to come again."

12

THE MERE WAY in which she entered the room told plainly that she had been waiting a long time, not only in the waiting room, but long before that, waiting to see Petit Louis at last, to be able to speak to him, to be able to get things straight.

She hardly faltered for a second on seeing him changed, grown fatter, with several days' growth of beard on his chin, in a shirt that had no collar, and looking more sullen than ever after hearing her name.

She came in from the outer world, cool from the autumn air, and brought with her a sort of distant echo of life outside, of streetcars and automobiles, of shopping crowds. She was clean and neat. She came forward impulsively.

"Monsieur Louis," she began, "I must tell you . . ."

Like a judge on the bench, Monsieur Monnerville rapped on his desk with a ruler, calling her to order.

"Mademoiselle! Would you mind turning toward me and not speaking to the prisoner."

"But why have they . . . ?"

"You can speak when I question you."

He had handled the Menton creature with kid gloves, but he was instantly up in arms against this eager girl.

"You stated to the police . . ."

"Monsieur Magistrate, I swear . . ."

"Silence! You stated to the police that you met Louis Bert on Tuesday, August 23, shortly before noon. He was carrying a rather large package and appeared embarrassed at seeing you. . . ."

Niuta's small fingers were quivering with impatience, her lips trembling with eagerness to speak.

"They asked me . . ."

"Never mind what they asked you. Do you stand by your statement? Did you on that Tuesday meet the . . ."

"I don't know."

And she looked at Petit Louis as though begging him to prompt her.

"I hope you realize the gravity of the question. The issue in this case is nothing less than murder, so take care what you say. In your statement . . ."

"I can't remember anything."

"Yet you seemed quite definite when you answered the police."

"They put the answers into my mouth."

"Among other things, you said that on the night of the 20th to the 21st of August you heard sounds of a quarrel in the apartment occupied by Madame Ropiquet and the accused. . . ."

Petit Louis pricked up his ears, suddenly interested. He had the dates clear in his mind by now, and the night in question was the one he spent in his brother-in-law's bar in Toulon.

"Do you hold to your statement?"

"No!"

"Mademoiselle, I must once more ask you to consider the seriousness of what you're saying."

"The police asked me if I'd ever heard any noise, and went on at me until I was quite mixed up."

Each time she spoke she glanced at Petit Louis, as though begging for some sign of approval.

"Then I must ask you something else. Can you assure me that

your relations with the prisoner have never been anything more than neighborly?"

Petit Louis's lips curled with disgust, while Niuta looked wide-eyed at the magistrate and then, when she understood, nearly burst into tears.

"Can you also tell me whether you live absolutely alone in Nice, without anybody to act as guardian and guide you, while your mother travels in America?"

Then, without giving her time to answer, he said:

"I'll send for you again when you've had time to reflect."

In the end, Petit Louis couldn't help regarding it with some-thing akin to admiration—that huge dossier that day by day grew ever bulkier, ever more exhaustive. In its pages, a whole population came forward to testify, often people whose existence he had forgotten, who now for a moment reappeared out of the past to say their little piece, to add one little touch to the portrait of the accused, like the man who said:

"He went off on a Saturday night without paying his bill."

That was a hotelkeeper who'd been brought all the way from Avignon, and the bill in question was for no more than forty-two or forty-three francs.

Almost every day now the same prison van, but with a differ-ent guard each time, took Petit Louis from the prison to the Palais de Justice. Only, instead of being ushered straight into Monsieur Monnerville's room, he was put into the one next door, formerly a coatroom, a small, badly lighted room, furnished with a bench. There he waited, sometimes a few minutes, sometimes a whole hour. Then the door would open and he would be pushed into the magistrate's presence, and sitting by the desk would be some new phantom from the past, a bus conductor, the innkeeper from Le Pradet, a man he'd played belote with at his brother-in-law's.

"Do you recognize the prisoner?" Monsieur Monnerville would ask, while Petit Louis remained standing.

"He's fatter, but that's him all right."

After which Petit Louis would be taken back to his bench in the next room. He had become a mere super, not even a spectator. He was left to guess what all these people said about him.

One day he found himself confronted by his former army sergeant, who had become a croupier in Juan-les-Pins.

Another time, two people were there, obviously from the country, a man and a woman whom he tried in vain to place. He couldn't possibly guess that a human leg had been fished up out of the lake at Thau, near Sète, and that a certain worthy grocer and his wife had thought they recognized in Petit Louis's photograph in the papers a man who'd come into their shop one evening carrying a bulky package and who had seemed to them a little queer.

There had been columns and columns about it in the newspapers. The couple had been brought to Nice to identify Petit Louis, who was duly paraded with three other men.

"Is the man you saw in your shop one of these four?"

The grocer looked inquiringly at his wife, and, getting no help from her, shook his head. It was she who finally pointed to one of the policemen in plain clothes.

"If it wasn't that I thought he was a bit taller, I'd have said it was that one. Though I think he had a little mustache like Charlie Chaplin's . . ."

So the evidence piled up. The examining magistrate and his clerk worked twelve hours a day, and under the former's instructions people were questioned on oath in every corner of France.

Once again he saw the fat women from the bar in Cagnes-sur-Mer where he had drunk whisky with the Englishmen.

"Are you," asked the magistrate, "prepared to state that this man left your bar with the other customers you had that night and drove off with them in one of the cars?"

They had been in great form that night behind the bar, but now they sat inertly, like two great slugs, looking stupidly at each other.

"Can you remember?" asked one of the other.

"I don't know that I can."

"Please answer me without consulting one another. Are you certain . . ."

"No. I couldn't be certain. You know how it is. . . . We were in a hurry to close."

It was really too bad! There had been scores and scores of witnesses, and, with the solitary exception of the grocer from Thau, they had all been positive even when they were making mistakes or telling lies.

Here, if anywhere, was a solid fact. Petit Louis had indeed left with the Englishmen. It was, moreover, a matter of considerable importance, for the magistrate was trying to establish that the crime had been committed that night.

Yet now these two fat creatures couldn't remember! They hesitated, they vacillated, awed by the examining magistrate.

And the police, who could rake up his army sergeant and a hotelkeeper who had sheltered him for a few nights long ago, had proved themselves incapable of finding two "GB" cars or their owners, who were obviously familiar figures along the Riviera.

But Petit Louis was used to it by now, and no longer got worked up. Mornings he spent quietly in his cell, hardly bothering to wonder whether or not he'd be required for duty, as he put it, at the Palais de Justice during the afternoon. Sometimes he joked with the polished, well-fed guards who escorted him, joked clumsily, sardonically, because his heart was full of bitterness. Then, in his little waiting room, he tried to hear what was going on on the other side of the door.

Once, he nearly lost his composure, and that was when he was suddenly brought face to face with two elderly spinsters, one of whom carried a lorgnette. He recognized them. Yes, he was sure he had seen them before, and he was no less sure that their presence was a major disaster. Yet, try as he might, he was unable to place them.

"Is that the man? Can you formally identify him?"

Questions that Monsieur Monnerville had repeated a hundred times already.

"What do you think, Thérèse?" asked one of them of her sister.

"That's him. If I could see his hands, I could say for certain."

Then Petit Louis knew. They were the two old maids from the glove shop, where he'd asked for rubber gloves but had only been able to get leather ones.

"Hold out your hands."

"Six and a half! That's it. Besides, I was struck by his thumb...."

And she drew back, aghast at the thought of being within arm's length of a murderer.

Another whom Petit Louis had forgotten was a barman, who, it must be admitted, was hesitant about recognizing him.

"He came in for a drink, but didn't seem to know what he wanted. Said something about a streetcar accident, and I told him that, the week before..."

And it was the slender, frail Monsieur Monnerville who had to carry this world upon his shoulders. For that's what it was: a whole world of evidence elaborately constructed from the bits and pieces provided by a world of witnesses. Big witnesses and little witnesses, tragic ones and fussy ones, old ones and young ones, right down to the old waxwork who lived opposite and who tottered into the examining magistrate's room just to say that he spent his life looking out of the window and hadn't noticed anything out of the ordinary! He was deaf into the bargain. The questions had to be written down, and he bawled out the answers.

And of all this world that Monsieur Monnerville carried on his shoulders Petit Louis was the axis.

Sometimes there were only a few witnesses. On other days they positively swarmed, and it looked as though an advertisement had been put in the papers: "Witness required. Apply to M. Monnerville. Room No. ..."

A salesman wrote from Bourges; a milkman from Calais had a

free trip to the Riviera to say at the end of it that he had never seen Petit Louis and that the man he'd been talking about had a scar on the left cheek. . . .

For three whole days it was nothing but dates and hours, and everybody, including the magistrate and Petit Louis, got mixed up. The same witnesses had to be recalled next day, when it was seen that their evidence didn't tally with the official timetable drawn up by Monsieur Monnerville. And that official timetable was wrong, absolutely wrong. Some witnesses were a day out, some a whole week!

Then, all of a sudden, a flat calm. For over a week Petit Louis was left in his cell, where the Yugoslav, having been sentenced to ten years, had surrendered his place to a crooked accountant who spluttered when he spoke. The spluttering soon stopped, however, when Petit Louis told him very firmly to keep his mouth shut.

At last, one morning, he was told that his lawyer was coming to see him, and the accountant was taken away. From having lived so long in Monsieur Monnerville's presence, Maître Bouteille seemed to have entered into the spirit of the case.

Unconsciously, he betrayed the well-earned satisfaction of a man who has accomplished a Herculean task, and it was in a tone almost of gaiety that he announced:

"Well! We've got through that. The case now goes to the Assizes. The final charges are: murder with premeditation, concealment of a dead body, theft, breach of trust, forgery, and using forgeries."

Laying his bursting briefcase on the table, he went on proudly:

"The dossier contains eight hundred and twenty-three documents, and two hundred and thirty-seven witnesses have been heard! Now we've got to talk things over seriously. Our case will be the big event of the next session. Without false modesty, I must tell you that I feel quite capable of undertaking your defense, though I did consider calling in one of the crack Paris criminal lawyers. . . ."

"You know I have no money."

"You don't seem to realize that at the present moment there isn't a lawyer worth mentioning who wouldn't jump at the opportunity of defending you for nothing. The case is even arousing curiosity abroad, and there will be more than one foreign correspondent at the trial. . . . No, it isn't that. . . . If I rejected the idea of appealing to counsel from Paris, it was because juries in Nice don't take very kindly to strangers butting in on what they regard as a local affair. I could quote you some recent examples. . . ."

Petit Louis looked at him as if he were some creature from another world. To hear him talk, you would think it was Maître Bouteille who was the principal figure in the drama; it was his case and it was his prowess that was to be put on trial.

"Yesterday, I discussed the matter with two lawyers here, the best in Nice, in my opinion, and both agreed to assist me. . . ."

"Well, if it's all fixed up . . ." said Petit Louis with indifference. "But when does it start?"

"Probably in June."

"What? Not before then?"

"We've none too much time. There's the whole of your defense to prepare. It's only now that the inquiry's over that we can really get down to it. Have you made any plans?"

"Plans? What for?"

"I suppose you realize by now that the case for the prosecution is absolutely devastating. Monsieur Monnerville is the most thorough examining magistrate of them all, and his integrity has never been questioned. What we have to decide is this: are we going to plead guilty but deny premeditation, and even claim extenuating circumstances, or are we going to flout the evidence and plead not guilty?"

"Of course we are."

"Listen, Petit Louis, between us, I may as well tell you frankly . . ."

No! Nothing of the kind! Petit Louis wasn't going to confess anything, neither to his lawyer, nor to his two pals, the "best lawyers in Nice," nor to anybody else. He'd made up his mind about that, once and for all, and he hardly listened to Maître Bouteille, who, he could see, was just dying for some sensational revelations, like any old busybody eager for scandal.

"Listen, Petit Louis! Can't you understand that your plan won't stand up?"

"It isn't a plan."

"Considering all they found against you . . ."

"Look here!" interrupted Petit Louis. "Couldn't you arrange for me to have something to do? I could make toys, penny whistles, anything you like. . . ."

He could no longer put up with a lot of chatter. It wore him out. The mere sight of this lawyer, fussy and talkative, made him feel sick.

"But we really must get down to . . ."

"Yes, yes! . . . Another time . . . Do you know what's happened to my mother?"

"One of the local reporters, whom I met in the Palais, took pity on her. She's working for him now."

This earned a nasty look from Petit Louis, who didn't like reporters any better than magistrates or lawyers. He wondered what this newspaperman hoped to get out of his mother in return for his kindness.

"I'll come and see you again as soon as . . ."

"So . . . And don't forget I want some work to do."

Work he did. And to everyone's surprise he did it calmly, purposefully, and with astonishing dexterity. From morning to evening he went at it without raising his eyes, without a word to his cellmate, making little toys of common pine as though his life depended on it.

It didn't keep him from putting on weight. And every day the look in his eyes became darker, duller, and more cautious. He seemed reluctant, almost afraid, to look at people or things. When he did so, it was with sly, furtive glances and sudden retreats, covered by rapid blinking.

Two or three times, the prison warden came to see him, puzzled by reports of his exemplary conduct. Another time, it was the chaplain, who complimented him on his skill. Petit Louis didn't answer, however; he merely looked at the man in the cassock as he looked at all the others, with mistrust, like someone who has lost all contact with his fellow men.

"Don't you think it would be a good thing, Petit Louis, if we had a heart-to-heart talk? It might comfort you...."

No answer. Just a look. And Petit Louis's hands went on busily with his work.

"I've seen your mother, who had let her religion slide all the time she was at Le Farlet, but who now finds it gives her strength to face her trouble...."

Another look from Petit Louis. Not a nice look at all. So in the end the chaplain had no choice but to beat a retreat, muttering, like the lawyer:

"I'll look in again.... I won't lose hope that ..."

The crooked accountant, who hated Petit Louis, couldn't let slip the opportunity of saying:

"They talk as though they were speaking to a condemned man!"

And nobody, nobody in the whole world, could have told what was going on behind Petit Louis's obdurate forehead, while his hands busied themselves with innocent work.

He knew he was alone, absolutely alone. That's why he wanted no help from anybody. And this feeling of solitude, far from discouraging him, charged him with energy.

Maître Bouteille wanted him to confess, to say:

"Yes, I did kill Constance Ropiquet, but save me, just the same! You must move heaven and earth to save my head...."

But he wasn't going to say that, or anything like it. He had summed them up, all of them, and judged them, and if anybody was going to save Petit Louis's head, it would be himself.

Weeks passed. He ate everything he was given and never complained. Now and then he stopped for a moment to joke with the ginger-haired guard with a nasal voice, whose face he liked better than the others'.

Maître Bouteille brought his two colleagues, the "best lawyers in Nice," and Petit Louis was at no more pains to be nice to them than he was for anybody else. He wasn't going to thank them with so much as a smile for undertaking his defense.

"You needn't bother about Petit Louis," he sneered. "They're not going to chop his head off. Not this time!"

This thought of a head cut off he could read in the eyes of all who came near him, and it became more and more visible as the date of the trial approached. The ginger-haired guard was more considerate than ever, and the lawyers brought him candy.

They all seemed to be saying to themselves:

"Poor fellow! He doesn't know what's coming to him!"

And Petit Louis glanced at them with those eyes of his that gave nothing away. Then, when they had gone, he returned to his thoughts, which, like his hands, never stopped. While everybody around him felt more nervous tension as the trial drew near, he became steadily calmer, until at last he enjoyed a peace he had never known before, with the possible exception of those mornings when he had lain in bed listening to Niuta in the next room singing Chopin's "Berceuse."

It had taken Monsieur Monnerville a little over two months to erect his monumental dossier, which passed, among those best able to judge, for a model of its kind. The lawyers were now going over it line by line, looking for holes.

But Petit Louis *knew*! He alone possessed the truth; he was the only one who knew the relatively simple reality that lay buried beneath the examining magistrate's edifice of learned reconstruction, the only one who knew that that imposing piece of architecture was absolutely false. The dates were wrong, and then, to patch things up, witnesses had been harried until they'd lost their way, confused a Sunday with a Monday or one week with another, but had nevertheless finally given an answer that fitted into the official timetable established by Monsieur Monnerville. No doubt the latter was acting in good faith, but he must now and then have been troubled by an inner voice that asked whether things had really happened in the way he wanted them to happen.

In short, Monsieur Monnerville had reconstructed the crime according to his own idea, and it was that crime, not the real one, that was to go before the Assizes.

"If you get any fatter," said the ginger-haired guard, laughing, "the witnesses won't be able to say it's you."

Petit Louis hadn't joined in the laugh; he laughed no longer. The best he could do was a little grimace, which expressed an attenuated form of good humor.

"They're beginning to talk about your case again in the papers. There're going to be special tickets for admission, and so many reporters are coming that they're having to rearrange the seating. Extra telephones are being fixed up in the Palais for them. . . ."

Twice his lawyers had threatened to abandon the case if he refused to help them.

"I bet you can't," he had answered cynically.

Five days to go, then three, then two, and Petit Louis was as calm as ever. He saw to various little details, such as sending his suit to the cleaner's, getting a new tie and three shirts. For he had been told the trial would last three days, and they were right in the middle of summer.

On the day before, he sent for the prison barber, had his hair cut, and arranged for a shave first thing next morning.

On the other hand, when the lawyers showed him a whole pile of news stories, he didn't have the curiosity to read a single one, though he studied the photographs.

"That's not like me," he said scornfully.

Or:

"I wonder when they took that. . . . I don't even know where it is. . . ."

And then, without any transition:

"Will my mother be there?"

"She's down to give evidence."

"And Niuta?"

"Niuta, too."

"What about Louise?"

"She's been served with a summons, but she hasn't turned up yet."

"Good," he said.

And he started to clear up his little table, which for so many weeks had served as a carpenter's bench.

13

THE BARBER, who was there for having put five or six revolver shots into his fiancée, came along jauntily at six o'clock in a ray of sunshine.

"Do you know how many reporters there are?" he asked excitedly, as though it were his own trial or some big sports event. "Fifty-three!"

That was an exaggeration. There were only forty-nine, twenty of whom had arrived from Paris the night before. And in the great white hotels along the Promenade des Anglais the staff couldn't understand why such a lot of people were up so early.

Petit Louis couldn't see the Bay of Angels, which that morning was the color of lavender, a wide expanse, unbroken by a sail, unruffled by the slightest ripple, as far as the eye could see.

The Parisians enjoyed it to the full, and, on their way to the Palais de Justice, they made a detour to pass through the flower market, ablaze with carnations of every color.

The little bars had their early-morning smell of coffee, and the water cart ambled slowly through the streets, when forty men of the mounted police, on foot, but booted and helmeted, lined up on the monumental steps of the Palais.

Meanwhile, Petit Louis, who had dressed carefully for the occasion, was being jolted along in the narrow cell of the prison van, while the younger of his two guards eyed him with curiosity through the grating.

He was taken in through the little side door and put in a dismal gray room used for miscellaneous storage, in which a bench had been provided for him.

If it was quiet there, the rest of the Palais was buzzing with excitement. Men bustled about, looking important, like the stewards at a fete. Others stood outside on the steps, talking in groups. Below them were rows of parked cars and a crowd of people who stood gaping at the mounted police. Fashionable women arrived, some with passes, some without, the latter trying to gain admission by latching on to some reporter or lawyer.

In the court, the proprietor of a restaurant had left cards on the benches reserved for the press, having written below his name: "A hearty welcome extended to press representatives at specially reduced prices."

Petit Louis could hear little of all this, no more than a vague murmur and the occasional slamming of a door. He gazed at the young guard, suddenly realizing that he was strangely like him, particularly as he was now, with full cheeks and a smooth, taut skin.

Might he not just as well have been in the guard's shoes, and the latter in his? They both had the same wide, strong jaw and prominent cheekbones, the same eyes, the same forehead. . . .

One of the lawyers came in, already robed, and as excited as the barber had been that morning.

"Feeling all right? . . . Not too nervous?"

"Not a bit."

"Have you had a look at the court?"

He went over and opened a door a few inches, the one that led directly to the dock. Looking through, Petit Louis inspected the crowd, which was already thick, particularly at the back, where people were standing tightly packed. He caught the eyes of one or two people, and returned their stare without flinching.

"Has Louise come?" he asked the lawyer.

"Nobody seems to have seen her."

Petit Louis smiled sourly.

"And my sister?"

"She's not coming. She's sent a doctor's certificate."

What with diplomatic illness and all those whose evidence was worthless, the number of witnesses had been greatly reduced. All the same, there were still sixty-seven to be heard. In the court, people were getting impatient, because one of the jury members was late, and it was holding up the show.

Finally, everyone was in his place, the reporters having rushed in at the last minute from the neighboring bars. They went on with their conversations and even finished their cigarettes, in fact making themselves quite at home. The judges came in, and Petit Louis sat down in the dock, with all eyes turned on him and with cameras thrust under his very nose.

He smiled. Slowly and calmly, he surveyed the court, his eyes pausing for a moment when he caught sight of a face he knew. Automatically, his hand went up to adjust the knot of the blue bow tie with white spots he had chosen. Then he took out his handkerchief, because the palms of his hands were already clammy.

They started drawing names for the jury, and nobody bothered about him, not even his lawyers, who from time to time casually threw out the word "Exception," apparently objecting to somebody.

Since he was going to be there for three days, Petit Louis had to get used to the atmosphere. Already little details were engraving themselves on his memory, like the clock just above the court clerk, and the attitude of the assistant judge on the presiding judge's right, a big florid man who leaned back in his seat until he seemed almost to be lying down, and who appeared to be quite bewildered at finding himself where he was, seeing what he saw, and playing a part in so memorable an event.

While the indictment was being read, one of Petit Louis's lawyers, standing near him, pointed out the best known of the reporters. Petit Louis nodded his head at each name and studied their faces attentively. Meanwhile, the presiding judge was chatting with the assistant judge on his left, and the public prosecutor was patiently sorting out his papers.

The air that came through the tall windows still had some of its morning freshness. It wasn't until later that an old reporter complained of the draft and had them shut.

"Will the accused stand!"

They had been there a whole hour, and the trial was only just starting. Petit Louis stood up, his clammy hands resting on the light oak ledge that ran along the front of the dock. Before he spoke, the judge cleared his throat, preparing his voice in order to come in on the right note. He looked worried and suspicious, as though afraid his first words would unleash a burst of laughter or derisive hoots.

"Are you Louis Bert, born in Lille?"

"Yes, Monsieur President."

It was the first time his voice had been heard, and necks were craned to get a better look at him.

"Your father was a miner until he was mobilized on the outbreak of the war?"

"Yes, Monsieur President."

There wasn't a tremor in his voice. He held himself very erect, though without a hint of swagger, and his eyes looked straight into those of his questioner.

"When the Germans advanced on Lille, your mother, with you and your sister, took refuge in the South of France?"

"Yes, Monsieur President."

"There that unhappy woman did all in her power to give you a good upbringing, and all through your childhood you had nothing but good examples before you. . . ."

Petit Louis opened his mouth, but shut it again without saying anything. The judge noticed it and was incautious enough to ask:

"Did you wish to say something?"

Petit Louis looked directly at him. Everybody waited, but Petit Louis hadn't quite made up his mind. His Adam's apple moved and his fingers paled as he gripped the oak ledge.

"Yes, Monsieur President."

"The gentlemen of the jury are listening. Will you turn toward them?"

Petit Louis obeyed, but his eyes returned automatically to the judge.

"I wanted to say that during all our childhood, my sister and I slept in the same room, and in the next room my mother slept with old Dutto. And we knew exactly what was going on there."

He turned sharply toward the back of the court, where a lively murmur had broken out, and his eyes swept the rows of faces. The judge brought his ruler down with a bang on the desk before him.

"I had better say at once that I will tolerate no demonstration from any quarter."

The reporters were writing feverishly. Petit Louis, having had his say, seemed to sink back into himself.

"I consider it most regrettable that you should think it fit to speak in such a way of the unhappy woman whom we shall be seeing presently in the witness box. . . . Other witnesses, on whose honor I trust you will seek to cast no aspersions, will be coming to say that they have always regarded Madame Bert as a woman of saintly character, and they will also say that from your earliest childhood you have evinced instincts of the worst description. . . ."

Petit Louis's lips curled, and for a moment the judge remained in suspense, ready to plunge into a wrangling match with Petit Louis, as people wrangle in the street or in a café.

"You are, I suppose, prepared to admit that as a small boy you were more than once guilty of stealing?"

And, in a tone of condescension, Petit Louis answered:

"Yes, Monsieur President."

"You admit it?"

"Yes, yes. Of course I do, Monsieur President."

"Do you also admit that you were expelled from the school in Le Farlet?"

"Yes, Monsieur President."

"And that, at a young age, you began to indulge in sexual practices, frequenting houses of ill fame at an age when . . ."

"As soon as I could, Monsieur President."

This raised a laugh among the public, a laugh that was definitely in his favor, and the judge threatened once more to clear the court. It was then that he stated ponderously:

"I hope it will not be forgotten that the shadow of a dead woman broods over these proceedings!"

And the chief counsel for the defense took the opportunity to add: "Or that my client's life is at stake!"

Petit Louis looked at him in surprise, then shrugged his shoulders and turned back toward the judge, bracing himself for the next attack. The red robes on the bench did not impress him. The only thing that upset him was the fidgeting of the prosecutor, who never for one minute stopped twirling his white mustache. He felt like begging the man to keep still, because it got on his nerves and prevented him from giving his whole mind to the trial.

"I nevertheless take note of the fact that from an early age you were an assiduous customer of brothels."

It was Petit Louis's lawyer who added, in an audible aside:

"Like every other Frenchman!"

And Petit Louis smiled, while the judge, after a moment's hesitation, pretended he hadn't heard it.

"Later on, your dealings at these places took on another character, when you endeavored to make a living on the immoral earnings of their inmates. . . ."

"Monsieur President, I can see at least ten people in this court who make their living that way, yet nobody accuses them of having killed Constance Ropiquet."

There was a stir in the court as everyone turned to exchange

154

glances with his neighbor. The public prosecutor, coming to the judge's rescue, indignantly exclaimed:

"In all my long career at the bar I have never come across such brazen cynicism."

"Suppose they accused *you* of killing your mistress!"

"Silence! . . . Silence at the back there! . . . Otherwise, I'll clear the court at once. . . . The first person to make the least disturbance is to be removed at once. . . . Really! It's intolerable! One might think this is a fairground instead of a court of law!"

The judge, now thoroughly rattled, tried to pick up the thread of his ideas. And Petit Louis stood there quietly with the sad, grave look in his eyes of a bull waiting for the banderilla.

"I am surprised that a man in your situation would think of making jokes. . . . Still, that's your business; I have no doubt the jury will know what conclusion to draw from it. . . ."

As a matter of fact, Petit Louis hadn't dreamed of joking. He was there alone in the middle of all those people who were out for his blood. They were the stronger. They had been able for nearly a year to cut him off from the world while they worked up the case in their own fashion.

And it disgusted him that they should stoop to these mean, underhanded arguments, which didn't even hold water.

Why did they say that he had had nothing but good examples held up before him, when everybody knew that Dutto was a dirty old man who had tried his dirty tricks on every little girl of the village, including Petit Louis's sister?

There was another question he'd have liked to ask, since they talked so superciliously of certain establishments. The public had to have tickets to get into the court, which were issued by the authorities. How then did it come about that, in the first row, there were at least three proprietors of brothels, including the one at Hyères, while in the rows behind there were plenty of others in the same racket?

And the wives and daughters of magistrates were sitting on the same benches!

He remained calm. He had made up his mind once and for all

that he wasn't going to lose control of himself. There were only his hand gripping the oak ledge in front of him, and his Adam's apple moving up and down.

"When you met Madame Ropiquet, you realized at once the capital you could make out of that well-to-do lady's unfortunate passion."

"Madame Ropiquet was a kept woman," corrected Petit Louis.

"Madame Ropiquet was an honorable widow whose only failing was to masquerade under a high-sounding name, a failing I think we can regard as a very harmless one."

"Was it also a harmless failing to receive two thousand francs a month from an old man who's since committed suicide?"

He had learned of the suicide from his lawyer. He could almost read, had he been able to look over the shoulder of one of the reporters, what he was writing: ". . . the incredible effrontery of the accused, who . . ."

But why the hell should they make everybody else out to be a saint, and he the only sinner?

That was just it! That was the whole case in a nutshell!

"I must warn the accused to keep his tongue in check, and in particular not to make aspersions against people who can no longer defend themselves."

The hands of the clock moved forward slowly, and after an hour's questioning Petit Louis was bathed in perspiration and his nostrils were pinched with fatigue. With the time of going to press in mind, the reporters slipped out one after the other to telephone their papers. Quite at ease, they came and went, offered each other candy, or filled their fountain pens.

"Do you admit that you left Madame Ropiquet at about midnight on August 19 at the Régence, where you had been dining with her?"

"Not alone."

"I didn't ask you that. Answer the question."

"Not only were we not alone," Petit Louis went on obstinately, "but a detective belonging to the Sûreté, who was certainly not there by accident, failed to make a complete report of the people present. I won't say any more about Monsieur Parpin, since you don't like it, but I'd like to ask Detective Mine what other persons were watching from outside. . . ."

"The question will be asked him when he takes his place in the witness box. . . . Why did you suddenly jump in a moving bus, and why did you equally suddenly jump off in the darkness?"

Petit Louis stubbornly remained silent. At that moment there was a slight stir in the courtroom among the men belonging to the underworld, who had certainly been sent there by Gène and the Marseille gang.

"We find you next in a bar that has none too good a reputation, where you perform a lot of tricks to amuse the other customers. And that goes on till three o'clock. . . . What did you do then? . . . I'll tell you. You came back to Nice and returned to Madame Ropiquet's apartment, to which you had a key. . . ."

"I went to Saint-Raphaël in one of the Englishmen's cars."

"Silence! You have no right to speak except when I give you permission. . . . You came back to Nice, where you committed the crime. Either Madame Ropiquet wasn't generous enough to satisfy your greed, or she may have tired of her liaison with you. Anyhow, you threatened her, and finally killed her, pocketing . . ."

"No, Monsieur President, you're on the wrong track."

Petit Louis seemed quite distressed, and it was in the same deprecating tone that he went on:

"You don't seem to have the faintest idea what happened. To begin with, Constance hadn't had enough of me. On the contrary she was more attached to me than ever. So much so that she even introduced me as her nephew to her old lover, and we all had dinner together, with Louise Mazzone. You see, it was her birthday. . . ."

"Quite a family party," the judge said ironically.

"If I had wanted to take anything, I only had to do it, since I had the run of the place and was often there alone. What would I want to kill her for?"

"The fact remains that you did kill her. If not, how do you explain that a few days later you were in possession not only of her mink coat but also of her papers, including her identity card?"

A moment's silence, then Petit Louis snapped:

"And her jewels?"

"What jewels?" asked the judge, taken aback.

"She didn't only have a fur coat. She had quite a lot of jewels, and she kept them in the apartment. What could I have done with them? . . . Since you soon tracked down everything else, how is it you didn't find them? Particularly since all jewelers are informers. . . ."

"I beg you . . ."

Petit Louis made a gesture, as much as to say:

"All right. Let it go. . . . Though you know very well it's true."

And he went on:

"There was money in the apartment, too. Louise Mazzone can confirm that. And if I'd killed Madame Ropiquet, I would have had that money, wouldn't I? In which case I wouldn't have had to snatch a lady's bag next day on the Promenade des Anglais. . . ."

All eyes opened wide. The judge bristled.

"Excuse me, but are you now boasting of a crime with which you're not even charged?"

"They never asked me about it. For that matter, they never asked me anything except a lot of silly questions about what I did when I was little, or just what time I got on a bus."

His lawyer shook his head disapprovingly. Petit Louis's hand dived into a pocket and produced the little medal bearing the head of St. Christopher.

"Here you are! This medal was in the bag, and three hundred francs. Afterward I threw the bag into the sea. If you put an advertisement in the papers, you'd soon get hold of the lady it belongs to. And she could tell you . . ."

The public watched breathlessly, hoping for another exchange between Petit Louis and the judge, who was beginning to lose his grip. Once more the prosecutor intervened.

"I protest against the introduction of new matter at this stage. Its only object can be to create a diversion and impede the trial. The accused has had ample time, during the preliminary inquiry..."

"Except that they never let me speak."

"Silence!"

But by this time the judge was completely flustered and, after consulting his notes in vain, he preferred to adjourn the trial for a quarter of an hour, which gave everybody the opportunity to dash out for a drink.

Many went out of their way to pass close to the dock, to have a good look at Petit Louis. One of them was the proprietor of the house at Hyères, who winked at him as he passed.

That evening, after the second session, one of the Paris reporters, who specialized in criminal cases, declared as he gathered up his papers:

"He'll get twenty years."

Noisily, the crowd dispersed, and Petit Louis was taken back to his cell, where the crooked accountant looked sourly at him, jealous of his celebrity.

Next day, in the dingy gray waiting room, Petit Louis glanced through the newspapers his lawyer had brought along. "To the questions asked him by the judge, the accused answered with revolting callousness," he read.

"There you are!" said the lawyer. "I knew you'd turn opinion against you."

"Haven't they found Louise yet?"

"They've telegraphed all over the place, but they can't find out her present address."

As if the police could be unable to locate a registered prostitute! Of course they could put their hands on her at any moment they wanted to.

The truth was they didn't want her there. Under cross-examination, she might make some damaging admission. They preferred this long string of squalid witnesses who could rake up every petty misdeed of his boyhood.

One after the other they passed through the witness box.

Petit Louis didn't stir the whole time. He looked them in the eye, just as he had the judge.

"Raise your right hand . . . Say 'I solemnly swear . . .' "

"I solemnly swear . . ."

There was even a grocerywoman who thought she had seen Petit Louis in Le Farlet, sneaking around with an enormous package.

"Say 'I solemnly swear . . .' "

She solemnly swore. But in the end she got mixed up on her dates and, when the lawyer asked her specific questions, she admitted that the meeting she had mentioned had actually taken place on the eve of the fete in Le Farlet, a good month before the death of Madame Ropiquet.

A taxi driver also got his dates mixed up. He claimed to have taken Petit Louis to the Villa Carnot, along with a large trunk of an unusual design. He was a Russian with a heavy accent. Petit Louis studied him and was sure that he had never met him.

"What makes you think, a year later, that the events that you recall took place on August 21?"

"Because it was a Saturday and on Sunday I went to Monte Carlo, where I had a breakdown. I found the bill from the garage. . . ."

"You say it was a Saturday?"

"I'm sure of it!"

"Then it wasn't August 21, which fell on a Monday!"

It went on and on. The two old spinsters who kept the glove shop amused the spectators by getting angry with the photographers. The reporters sat back and doodled in their notebooks to pass the time. It was only Petit Louis whose attention never wandered for a second, and he leaned over to his lawyers now and then to prompt them in a whisper.

When the turn came for the seedy Minable to give evidence, Petit Louis could hardly remain in his seat, and his face was tense with expectancy.

"Do you swear to tell the truth, the whole truth, and nothing but the truth?"

"I swear."

And he cast a little glance, just one and only one, at Petit Louis.

"Tell us what you know of the Ropiquet case."

"In my capacity as a detective of the Sûreté, I have not been particularly concerned with this case. It happened, however, that one evening when I was off duty—that is to say on the night of Friday, August 19—I was sitting in the café of the Régence when I saw Petit Louis in the company of other people. . . ."

"How many people?" asked the counsel for the defense.

The judge called him to order at once.

"I must request you, Maître, not to address the witness, but to put your questions through me in the proper manner."

Then, turning to the witness:

"How many people were with Petit Louis?"

The veins stood out on Petit Louis's temples, as he leaned forward eagerly, with his elbows on the ledge.

"Three."

Petit Louis whispered to his lawyer, who rose to his feet again.

"Monsieur President, would you ask the witness how he came to recognize Petit Louis?"

"The witness may answer."

The yellow-toothed Minable looked around him rather uneasily.

"My duties had brought me in contact with him in the course of another inquiry."

"Can the witness tell us what that inquiry was?"

"I believe . . . I think I ought to plead professional secrecy, because that inquiry is not yet terminated."

"Unless that other case has a bearing on the one we are now trying?"

Petit Louis's head was thrust forward, his eyes staring hard at the witness, as though to compel him to speak the truth.

"I don't think it has."

"You're not sure?"

"The witness," declared the judge, "is entitled by his occupation to invoke the plea of professional secrecy."

Petit Louis sprang to his feet.

"Will the accused kindly remain seated. . . ."

"But . . ."

"Sit down!"

At that moment those who were nearest to Petit Louis might have detected a tear in his eye, the first, and the last, too, a tear of helpless rage.

The man who could have saved him was there within a few yards of him in the middle of the reporters and photographers. He stood there in his best suit, his hat in his hand, and with the shamefaced look in his eye of one who has been called upon to play a part he knows very well is none too clean.

The judge, sensing the danger, asked:

"Any more questions?"

Petit Louis grabbed his lawyer by the shoulder and spoke to him in a voluble undertone, while his eyes never left the seedy Minable, at whom he gazed with such fury that he seemed ready to spring at his throat.

"Yes. Will the witness tell us what the accused said to him that evening?"

"I don't remember very precisely. I was off duty at the time and didn't take much notice. . . . I think he said something about some people being after him, but I really can't say for certain."

"Did he mention any names?"

"I don't remember any."

"Was he referring to people who had come under suspicion in the other case that was mentioned just now?"

"As I said before, that other case is still under investigation, and I must ask permission not to answer that question."

"Quite right," put in the prosecutor.

"Do the members of the jury wish me to ask the witness any further questions? . . . Very well! Before you go, Monsieur Mine, the court would like to thank you for your evidence and compliment you on your professional probity."

Petit Louis snorted. He snorted as loudly as he could, and it was meant, not only for the judge and the witness, but for everybody else as well. Then he hid his head in his hands and remained like that for a good ten minutes. He wasn't weeping. Perhaps he wasn't even thinking.

When he looked up again, there was a different expression on his face, an expression of complete indifference to all that was going on around him. His mind wandered, as it had at school, and he followed the movements of a fly, or idly watched the patterns traced by one of the reporters on the paper in front of him.

A little shudder went through the court when the electric iron was produced, the fatal piece of material evidence, on which the whole case hinged, yet Petit Louis merely gave it a casual glance.

Experts had examined it, and they came forward one after another to tell their conclusions. And Petit Louis hardly bothered to listen to what they said. It didn't matter now.

"Will the witness tell us whether this electric iron could have been used for the purpose of . . ."

It was pitiful to see all these people with ridiculous solemnity reconstructing a crime that had never been committed. Some of them tried to be witty, and were called to order.

"Do not forget, gentlemen, that the shadow of a dead woman . . ."

Nobody felt the presence of that shadow. In fact, nobody felt anything at all. Now that the last skirmish was over, the trial had become monotonous, and Petit Louis even heard one of the reporters say to his lawyers:

"Try to provoke a nice little scene about three o'clock—to give me a headline for the third edition."

A lot of fuss was made over Madame Bert when she went into the witness box. The judge was full of consideration.

"I very much regret, Madame, that you have to undergo this additional ordeal. . . ."

A chair was produced for her, and the photographers were requested to spare her. She was bewildered by her surroundings and didn't know which way to face. She hadn't even caught sight of Petit Louis. As for him, he gazed intently at her, with eyes that were dry.

"I must ask you to make an effort and tell the gentlemen of the jury—turn that way please—what you know of this painful subject. . . ."

"What do you expect me to say? I'm a most unlucky woman, and I can't think what I've done for God to punish me in this way. . . . If it wasn't that one of the newspaper gentlemen has kindly taken me on to do his housework . . . If only my poor old legs will stand it . . . And now what are you going to do with my son?"

"What the jury would like to know is whether, when your son came to see you on Saturday, August 20, he made an unfavorable impression on you. . . ."

"How should I know, with that old miser Dutto lying there at death's door? . . . Perhaps we did have a little argument. . . ."

She spoke in the thin plaintive voice of an old woman.

"Where is he?" she went on. "I don't believe he did it. . . . It wasn't from either his father or his mother that he learned to live a bad life. . . ."

She sniffled, then wept, too overawed by the court even to look in her bag for her handkerchief.

"No! . . . I'm sure he didn't do it. . . ."

Apart from her ravaged face, she was just a bundle of black clothes that smelled of mothballs. The judge exchanged glances with the prosecutor.

"I don't think we need prolong this painful scene any further. You can leave the witness box, Madame Bert. Guard! Help the witness out. . . ."

Until she was within a yard of the door, Petit Louis didn't move a muscle. Then he got up and, looking calmly and defiantly across the court, said in a clear voice:

"Mama, I swear I didn't kill her!"

She wanted to come back to him, but she was led out, while the judge explained:

"Madame Bert will be given an opportunity of seeing her son during the adjournment."

The trial went on. One of the lawyers had brought some sourballs, and from time to time he handed one to Petit Louis. After the adjournment, the judge had two of the same candies, wrapped in pink paper, on his pile of papers.

"Twenty years!" repeated the Paris reporter. "You'll see!"

There was even some betting on it.

The Orléans lawyer gave evidence, followed by the girl from the brothel in Menton and the one from the post office there, and then the concierge of the Villa Carnot.

Niuta didn't appear. She had sent a telegram from Salzburg, where she was with her mother, to say she was unable to attend.

Two or three times, out of sheer disgust, Petit Louis nearly got up and blurted out:

"The body's lying in two halves on the bottom of the harbor. . . ."

Then what? . . . The trial would be suspended, and another interminable inquiry would start.

His lawyer said hopefully:

"We may get an acquittal on the murder charge. But they'll pitch into you for all they're worth on the other charges. . . . Five or ten years . . ."

As the proceedings dragged on, Petit Louis's attitude became more and more that of a mere spectator. Particularly when they spoke of Constance, Louise, and the Villa Carnot, and the events of the previous year, he found it difficult to believe that he had really lived through all that.

Finally he was quite at a loss to know how and why it had all happened. Suddenly he said to his lawyer:

"He makes me sick."

He was actually referring to the judge, but it was equally true of the rest of them, especially the prosecutor and his silly white mustache.

What did they look like out of their robes? And what sort of men would they be in their own homes?

The stream of witnesses flowed on like water under a bridge. Toward the end of the third day, there were still thirteen left, which was a nuisance, because the next day was Sunday and they had decided to finish the case before that.

They were hurried into the witness box, sworn in, asked a perfunctory question or two, then hurried away again, so that the last pieces of evidence were given at a gallop.

And Petit Louis sat there, all alone, his face calm and contemptuous. At one moment his thoughts had wandered so far that he was regretting not having given his ring to the little servant in Porquerolles, to save it from falling into the hands of the law.

He was twenty-five. Occasionally, with a frown, he examined the faces of the jury one by one. After all, he couldn't quite throw off fear of the executioner.

Hadn't his lawyer been lying when he'd spoken of five or ten years? They were all lying in one way or another. They were so smug, horribly smug. In the presence of Petit Louis, who was charged with all the sins possible to human frailty, they seemed to find it necessary to congratulate themselves and each other on their honesty, their conscientiousness, and their professional integrity....

They knew that the case against him was full of holes, that on the main question, the only one that really mattered, the question of the murder of Constance Ropiquet, they had not the shadow of proof. They hadn't even been able to produce a body.

But the holes were richly plastered over with any sort of mud that came to hand, from petty larceny to brothels.

"Don't you think it would be a good thing to . . ."

And to his lawyer, too, Petit Louis answered:

"You make me sick."

When the public prosecutor finally summed up the case for the prosecution, he seemed, as he paused at the end of each sentence, to be inviting applause. By the time he had finished, with the inevitable demand for the death sentence, he was red in the face, and there were beads of perspiration on his balding head.

He drank a glass of water. One of Petit Louis's lawyers spoke, then another. And Petit Louis contemplated the crowd of spectators, which had been reinforced by more people, from Heaven knows where, until it was a compact mass of perspiring humanity.

When at last the fatal questions were put to the jury, it was eight o'clock, and the lights had to be switched on. His lawyers had no time now to think of Petit Louis. They darted hither and thither, buttonholing first one reporter, then another.

"When are you leaving?"

"I'm in no hurry."

"Then let's have dinner together."

"I'll have to phone my paper first."

"Twenty years! I said so right from the start."

"You still think so?"

What was the good of setting in motion all the elaborate machinery of the law, of summoning people from far and wide, of filling eight hundred and something sheets with neat handwriting, with all the signatures duly attested . . . only to end up with this sorry piece of chicanery?

"Do you come from the North, too?" asked Petit Louis of one of his guards.

"From Valenciennes."

"I was born up there, but I've never been back, never farther north than Lyon."

He didn't want to think. Yet at that very time the jury was

deciding his fate. What would they say? . . . Never mind! They were bound to go wrong, since the whole case was faked.

Since the seedy Minable had refused to say . . .

So, having nothing to go on, they kept on repeating:

"He's a filthy little villain! Obviously he did it!"

Petit Louis had been taken back to the dingy gray waiting room. Now and then, as a door opened, he heard a hum of voices and pricked up his ears. Then once more he would sink back into himself.

"Have you got a cigarette?" he asked the guard from Valenciennes.

If they had let him, he'd have stretched himself out full length on his bench, and he wouldn't have budged even to go back and hear the verdict.

"If you only knew how sick they make me with all their talk!"

Sick. That was the only word to describe his feelings. He harbored no grudge against Gène and the others, who were no doubt sitting in a bar nearby with glasses of *pastis*, waiting to hear the verdict. He didn't even think too harshly of Louise. Admittedly, she was a bitch, but he ought to have known that from the start.

No. What bored him were these people who talked and talked till it made you feel sick. They must have known their case was thin. They must have made excuses to themselves. And whenever they came to a particularly threadbare patch, they used a lot of legal phraseology to show their great respect for justice.

"That's it!" said the guard as a bell rang.

This time the spectators didn't bother to sit down. They were all standing, including the reporters, and there was an atmosphere of departure, which foreshadowed the helter-skelter dispersal, to rush to telephones or cafés, or home to dinner.

"The answer to the first question is yes. The answer to the second question is yes. The answer . . ."

Never, perhaps, in his whole life had Petit Louis been so calm, so clearheaded, and he noticed that the judge had a tiny white speck on his right eye.

His lawyer turned toward him.

"They've said no to premeditation. . . . That saves your head."

"Oh!"

They told him that now, as though it was something altogether unhoped for, as though it had been an understood thing all along that he was to be condemned to death.

"I suppose I did her in by accident!" he sneered in an audible voice, and all heads were suddenly turned toward him.

He had resumed his rough, gangster tone of voice.

"After due deliberation, the court condemns you . . ."

The reporters turned, grinning, toward the man who had predicted twenty years.

The judge's voice went on solemnly:

". . . to twenty years' penal servitude and the loss of civil rights. . . ."

Petit Louis's lawyers looked pleased with themselves, as though they'd pulled off a difficult job.

"Is there anything the accused wishes to say?"

Petit Louis looked around at the people's faces, which were now lighted up by the old-fashioned chandeliers, though parts of the court were in shadow. Some of them, already making for the door, stopped to hear his answer.

And quietly, gently, with a strange smile, he replied:

"No, Monsieur President."

And he said it in such a way that roles were suddenly reversed, and it was they, the whole lot of them, the judges, the jury, the reporters, the smartly dressed women, all of them, including the counsel for the defense, who all at once found they had something urgent to do, somewhere to go, someone they had to speak to, because there wasn't a single one of them who had anything to be proud of.

So much so that, apart from the two guards, nobody bothered any more about Petit Louis. It was the one from Valenciennes who murmured philosophically:

"After all! . . . You're young. . . . You'll be only forty-five when you come out. . . . You really can't complain. . . ."

Isola de Pescatore
August 1937